TEMPTED

THE ASPEN SERIES
BOOK SEVEN

CINDY STARK

OLIVERHEBERBOOKS

Published by Oliver-Heber Books

0 9 8 7 6 5 4 3 2 1

 Created with Vellum

1

Hushed moonlight filtered down on Noelle Parker as she tucked her flirty lavender skirt beneath her and sat on a swing in the deserted town park. She pushed off, setting the swing in motion, letting the cool September air tease her legs while she waited for her boyfriend.

Ian hadn't arrived yet. He'd phoned a few hours ago, asking her to meet him at the park in Aspen's town square. He was on his way back to town after a two-week job in Wyoming and needed to see her.

She'd missed him, but she had to wonder why he'd insisted on the park and not her house. Something was up. Nervous jitters rattled through her as the chains that held the swing creaked. He'd sounded anxious on the phone, and the way he'd asked to meet her made it seem serious.

She wasn't ready for this. Wasn't ready for whatever he had on his mind.

He'd ask her to marry him, or he'd break up with her again. She wasn't prepared for either, and she didn't understand why he had to hurry things. He was the one who'd always said he wanted to take it slow.

Headlights appeared and drew closer. A moment later, the truck slowed and then parked next to her old Mustang. Her nerves twisted into a painful knot as she stood and walked over to meet him.

Ian climbed from his truck. His cowboy hat covered his blond hair and shielded his features from the ambient lighting that might have provided a clue to his mood.

"Wow," he said as he reached her. "Don't you look pretty?"

He'd been so cryptic about their meeting, and she'd known one way or the other that she'd need to be at the top of her game, so she'd done her best to look nice.

"Thanks." She stood on tiptoe to kiss him, and he gave her a light brush with his lips. After two weeks apart, the lack of intensity in his kiss spoke volumes. She tried to breathe through the pain of the emotional dagger slicing through her heart.

And she'd thought he might propose. What a joke.

"Noelle, there's—"

"Don't." She stepped from him and turned away. "If you're done, then just leave. Let's not go through this again. My heart can't take it."

Ian grasped her hand. She tried to pull away, but he wouldn't release her. "I don't want to hurt you, Noelle."

She pressed her lips together until they stopped trembling. She would not fall apart in front of him again. Or anyone, ever. Not over a broken heart.

First Ian, then Tyler. Now Ian again. She had to stop her madness.

She inhaled and met his gaze. "You're not hurting me. To do that would mean I fell for you once again, that I believed your promises. I'm not that naïve."

"Noelle."

The concern in his voice reached for her, and she mentally slapped it away. "Really, Ian. We've been doomed from the start. What is it this time? I'm demanding too much of your time? You need to find yourself?"

"I met someone."

"Oh, God."

The bottom dropped from her heart, and she scrambled to keep it from shattering on the ground. Too late, she realized as tears gathered in her eyes.

"She lives in Rock Springs. I'm transferring, moving tomorrow."

He'd obviously planned this for some time. Transfers within his company didn't happen overnight. "Well...that's..."

She could no longer form words. There was nothing left to say, she realized. She couldn't ask him if he was sure. Couldn't do anything.

If he'd looked for and found someone else, he didn't love her any longer. Maybe he never had.

She turned and hurried across the graveled lot to her car, not able to think beyond her next step.

"Noelle," he called out, but she didn't stop.

Everything inside her had withered, and she needed to escape before her heartbreak left her with nothing but a hollow shell. She clung to that thought as she entered her car, started the engine, and smashed the gas pedal, spitting rock and dust in his direction.

She hoped he choked on it.

————

The following morning came too early, and yet not early enough for Noelle. The blessed relief she might have received during sleep had eluded her. Her eyelids were stiff and swollen, and despite her attempts, cold water and several cups of strong coffee did not improve the dark shadows beneath her eyes.

She seriously considered calling her business partner and asking April to cover for her. But that would require April to make accommodations with her babysitter for April to get to their coffee shop earlier. Not to mention, Noelle knew from experience, the surest way into depression for her was to sit idly and pour over her troubles.

She needed to move, needed to stay busy. So, she gathered her things and headed for her car.

When she turned the key, the engine in her Mustang hesitated, but finally turned over. When she'd purchased the cute, but run-down red convertible a year ago, Ian had promised to help her tune it up and get it running properly. She'd even saved up for a new paint job, but, as was Ian's custom, he'd failed to follow through on his promises.

At least she could finally leave it all in the past. She wouldn't have to worry about running into him in town and falling prey to her weakness when loneliness crept in.

She left her small, turn-of-the-century farmhouse in the dust and headed into the dewy summer morning. The sun barely crested the horizon as she traveled the two-lane into the heart of small-town Aspen. Her coffee shop, the one consistently good thing in her life, would save her. She'd make coffee, bake scones, and laugh with the customers.

Time would pass, and she'd survive this. Like she'd survived the other difficult times in her life. She knew how to be alone. She'd been that way for as long as she could remember.

A loud explosion startled her. Steering became difficult as a thump, thump sounded beneath her car. She gripped the wheel and struggled to maintain control as she pulled off to the side of the road.

Once the car had stopped, she took a breath, trying to calm her pounding heart, and climbed out of her car. A shredded tire hung from the rim.

"*Shit,*" she whispered and sagged against the side of her Mustang. Had the fates really conspired against her this time to steal her sanity?

She focused on the sweet morning air and then pulled the cell phone from her purse. She'd be damned if a tire and a worthless guy would be her demise.

Fifteen minutes later, Walt's bright yellow tow-truck arrived. He drove past, swung around, and backed up close to her Mustang.

"Morning," he said as he climbed down from the cab, his age and potbelly slowing his pace. "Looks like you have a bit of trouble."

"My tire blew out."

"Uh-huh." He adjusted his ball cap over his wiry gray hair and knelt next to the flat tire. She averted her eyes to avoid the crack showing at the top of his pants. "It blew the side right off," he said.

She loved Walt with his small-town ways and concerns, like she did most of the folks in Aspen, but right now, she had to hold back the "no-shit" retort that hovered on her lips. "Can you fix it?"

"Not this tire. It's done. Finito." He gripped the side of the car and pulled himself up. "You got a spare?"

"Tire? I think so." Didn't all cars carry a spare? She walked to the back and opened the trunk, but found nothing.

Walt followed and peered inside. "That's no good. Looks like I'll be towing you in."

Noelle frowned. "Isn't it under something in there?" With her previous car, the spare had been beneath the trunk carpeting.

"Not with this one." He ran a hand over his whiskers. "I'll call the tire shop in Pinecone to see if they have a replacement in stock. If so, I'll run into town and get it for you. It's going to cost you extra, though."

Of course. Didn't it always? "How much?"

He grinned. "Free coffee for two weeks?"

She shook her head and smiled. This was why she'd been determined to come back to Aspen after she'd turned eighteen. "How about for a month? I'll also kick in a hundred bucks for your time and gas."

"Nah. Two weeks ought to do it. I don't want to take advantage of you. But I'll take fifty if you insist, just so my missus doesn't make me retire 'cause I'm not making any money."

"Thanks, Walt."

She waited in the cab while he loaded her car, and then he drove her into town.

"I'd stop in front of your place," Walt said, "but it looks like your customers have already taken all the spaces."

Her customers? Hardly. Noelle eyed the sleek, silver pickup truck parked directly in front of her building and gritted her teeth. It was bad enough Kade Collier, newcomer to her little town, had to desecrate the field of wildflowers next to her coffee shop in order to build his precious motel. Now, he'd taken to stealing *her* customer parking.

"Don't worry about it. I can walk from your station," she said to Walt. It was only half a block, and it would give her time to rearrange her attitude before she stepped inside her shop. "Make sure you pop over in a bit. I'll have some coffee and cash waiting for you."

"Sure thing, darlin'. See you soon."

As Noelle made her way across the quiet street, she spotted the parking space usurper standing near the front entrance of his building, talking to April's husband, the supervisor of the project. Kade glanced over as she stepped onto the sidewalk, giving her a thorough appraisal that set her on edge.

Just because he had a ripped body, delicious brown eyes the color of her best coffee and a smile that could melt the frost off the small pond near her house in the dead of winter, didn't mean she wanted him to turn those eyes or that smile on her.

"Do you think you could find somewhere else to park?" She called out to him, turning his smile quizzical. "Like in front of your own building instead of mine?"

2

Noelle unlocked and entered her shop before Kade could respond to her unfriendly request, and a sick feeling washed over her.

"Ugh." Her voice echoed in the darkened building. She had to stop now. She did not want to be *that* person. The one who hated all men because the ones she knew were idiots, assholes, or both.

She flipped on the lights, shedding color on her cheery yellow coffeeshop. There had to be decent guys out there somewhere, even if she hadn't discovered one yet. Except Walt. He was decent. And April's husband, Seth, seemed to be an all-around good guy despite the rough patch of trouble he and her friend had endured before they'd married.

It seemed her best option would be to forget finding a good man and focus on what she could control. Coffee. Her garden. Friends. They made her happy, made life worth living.

And she'd start that very moment.

She tossed her purse in the backroom and fired up the coffeemaker.

When April arrived an hour later, Noelle had the music

blaring and freshly baked scones sitting in the display case. She'd just finished icing donuts and was about to make cherry-almond muffins.

April shot her an odd glance and lowered the music to a more professional level. "What's wrong?"

Noelle cast a quick glance in her direction before she focused on measuring flour. "Nothing. Why do you ask?"

She put a hand on her hip and tilted her head, her brown ponytail swinging as she did. "Because you always play Adele when you're trying to bury your feelings or when you'd like to bury somebody. So fess up."

Noelle frowned as cold emotion churned inside her, and she wondered where the heat had gone. Ian couldn't have scarred her that much, couldn't have left her only a frigid, broken heart. "Ian broke it off again."

"*Son of a bitch.*" April pursed her lips and shook her head as though it took all her reserve to keep from spewing what she really thought. She closed the distance between them and wrapped her arms around Noelle.

Some warmth filtered through, comforting her, and let her know Ian hadn't entirely destroyed her feelings.

April searched her eyes. "I want to kill the bastard. How dare he mess with your heart like this?"

Noelle tried to resurrect an equal amount of disdain, but an aching emptiness echoed through her instead. "It's okay. We were doomed from the start. You and I both know that."

April shook her head. "No. Don't let him off so easily. When you gave him another chance, he promised. Do you remember that? You didn't want to date him, but he swore up and down he loved you, and that he'd been afraid of commitment. *That bastard.*"

Noelle could have ranted, too, but what would be the point? She focused on the cherries she added to the batter as though his choice didn't affect her. "He doesn't have a problem with commitment. Just a commitment to me. He found someone else."

That stopped April's tirade, much the way the same words had put a bullet through her heart the previous night and killed her love for Ian.

Somber compassion stole her features. "Oh, God. I'm so sorry, Noelle."

She managed a small snort. "To top it off, my tire blew out on the way to work." If she didn't laugh about it, she'd cry, and she was so done with crying.

April dropped her jaw. "You're kidding."

She shook her head. "Blew out the whole sidewall. Walt has it at his shop. He's trying to find a replacement in Pinecone."

"That's just...messed up, girl. Are you going to be okay?"

Before she could answer, the door chimed and the very first friend she'd made when she'd arrived in Aspen walked in. Kimber met her gaze, and her green eyes were wide with worry. "I saw your car across the street as I was heading to work. What happened?"

"Tire blew out," April said. "And Ian dumped her."

Noelle narrowed her eyes at her business partner. "Thanks for summing up my miseries in one short sentence."

Kimber frowned as she joined the two women behind the counter and took Noelle's hand. "He needs to pay."

"Right?" April added.

Kimber nodded. "You know, I'm a perfect shot when it comes to getting revenge. Eggs. Firecrackers. You remember, right?" she asked with a straight face.

Noelle couldn't help but smile as she left the front area to place the muffins in the oven. Kimber's dad had busted them both the year they'd turned nineteen. They'd thrown eggs at Johnnie Thompson's truck before they'd lit a boatload of firecrackers, tossed them under his vehicle, and ran. They were lucky they hadn't caught his truck on fire and blown the tank.

At the time, Noelle might not have cared if that had happened. She'd listened to Johnnie's sweet words, let him steal her virginity, and he'd flat out ignored her the following day. Losing her virginity had somehow made her invisible to him and had stolen the last of her innocence.

She and Kimber had agreed. The injustice required revenge.

Kimber's dad locked them both in the small cell inside City Hall. No need to notify anyone. The sheriff knew where his daughter was, and Noelle was on her own by then.

A chilly night in the slammer had cemented their friendship forever.

She returned to the front counter where her friends waited. "We couldn't even if I agree to your schemes. He's gone."

"Gone?" April asked.

"We'll wait for him to get back then. Seriously, I'm not above it." Kimber folded her arms, her expression mirroring her words.

Noelle shook her head, loving her friends dearly. "Gone, as in, he's probably already packed his stuff and moved to Wyoming with his new love."

Kimber blew out a breath and sagged against the counter. "Well, that takes the fun out of everything. I'm sorry, Noelle."

"You're better off without him," April added. "I wish we knew the girl's name so we could warn her."

Noelle shrugged. "Maybe he really loves her."

April grabbed one of the shop's spring green aprons and tied it around her. "If you ask me, the man is incapable of respectable emotions."

The neon pink logo on her apron flashed at Noelle. *Rumors.* Her shop. She'd built it from the ground up. April had recently joined her as a partner, but Noelle had come up with the idea.

She'd saved what money she could, and she'd begged the banker in Pinecone to lend her the rest.

She still believed to this day, the carafe of coffee and cranberry-orange muffin she'd taken him had been what had sold him on the idea.

Rumors was her baby and her love. Who needed a man, anyway? "I no longer care. I'm over him. We obviously weren't really in love in the first place." It didn't matter that he'd left a dark hole in her heart. No one could see it. Therefore, it didn't exist. She'd keep pretending until it became the truth.

"I know what you need," Kimber said, filling a cup with coffee. "Another man. A real man. Not a boy who toys with women's hearts."

She rolled her eyes. "I don't think so." She'd had enough of the male species for a while.

"Kimber's right," April added. "You know the saying about getting back on a horse after being bucked off."

Noelle slid the tray of donuts into the case. "No. What I need is to learn to take care of myself. For instance, I should have had a spare tire in my car this morning, and I need to know how to change it, too."

The front door chimed, and all three women looked up. None other than Kade Collier walked through the door. As he approached the counter with his ripped jeans, Mustang t-shirt, and a dark shadow enhancing his chiseled jaw, Noelle turned away. "I'll be in the back," she said to her friends.

"Wait a minute," Kade called out to her.

She paused for a split second before she continued walking. Whatever he had to say, she didn't care to hear. She stopped inside the backroom, out of sight, but where she could still listen to what he said.

"Good morning, Kade," April said. "Your usual?"

"Sure. But I was really hoping to talk to your partner, too."

"Noelle?" April asked in an innocent voice.

"Yes, Noelle," he responded. "Is she available?"

He knew damn well she'd ignored him and had gone into the backroom. She'd made it clear that she didn't care to speak to him.

The room grew quiet for a moment, and Noelle could sense the awkwardness from her distance.

"She's...busy," April finally responded. "Could I give her a message?"

He scoffed. "I just saw her. I only need a minute."

Noelle had conversed little with the man. Usually, the other construction workers came over and took coffee back to whoever else was at the site. She didn't know why he was bothering with her now. He sounded like a man who was used to getting his way, but he wouldn't this time.

The timer dinged, startling her, and she pulled the muffins from the oven.

"She's not talking to guys today," Kimber said.

Noelle cringed. Had her friend seriously said that?

"Guys?" Kade questioned.

"People," April responded. "Is there something I can help you with?"

Cade cleared his throat. "Kimber said guys. Does she have something against men, or just me?" He asked his last question with a hint of sarcasm.

Noelle rolled her eyes and exhaled a deep breath. Why couldn't he take a hint and just go away?

She stepped around the corner, and he turned his sultry-brown gaze to her. She wiped her hands on her apron as though he'd interrupted a very important task. "What can I help you with, Mr. Collier?"

3

Kade stared at the blond bombshell, regarded the annoyance simmering in her beautiful blue eyes as she waited for his answer, and he smiled. Apparently, he'd done something to catch the attention of the lovely coffee shop owner, and he wasn't about to miss the opportunity to talk to her.

Even if they weren't on the best of terms.

"I came to apologize, Miss Parker." He knew her first name, though he didn't use it. Knew quite a bit about her, actually. The fine citizens of Aspen were quick to talk about anything of interest, and he definitely found the woman interesting. But he'd play her game.

April and Kimber turned their gazes to Noelle, and she widened her eyes.

He kept his satisfaction to himself. "I should have realized I might affect business by parking in front of your shop. If the construction mess has affected your sales, I apologize for that. I'd hate to start our relationship on the wrong foot."

"Our relationship?" Noelle seemed surprised by his friendly attitude, as though she'd expected him to fight back.

And he was. She just didn't know it yet.

"No apology necessary," April said before he could play his next card. "With all the workers coming in from next door, our business has nearly doubled. You have our thanks."

"Is that so?" He switched his gaze to Noelle. "Good, then."

She stared at him for a long moment, causing his heart to thud in his chest. If only he knew her well enough to predict her next move. She intrigued him, despite the months of trying to ignore her.

But he'd noticed her every morning and every afternoon for weeks, coming and going from her shop. He'd been certain it would have taken him years to look at another woman after the heartbreak he'd recently endured. But Noelle Parker had ensnared him instantly.

His interest had started when he'd asked his construction supervisor if he knew her, if she was available. Seth Moore had responded that she wasn't married, and Kade's interest had grown from there. He'd heard she had a boyfriend, but he hadn't seen him show up around the shop once, and that said a hell of a lot.

Noelle glanced past his shoulder and then looked back at him. "If you'll excuse me, I need to talk to Walt about my car."

Kade turned and saw the friendly, gas-station owner headed toward Rumors. "Do you have a problem with it?"

She didn't answer, didn't give him a second glance as she headed out the front door, meeting the man on the sidewalk.

"I'm sorry, Kade," April said as she handed his coffee to him. "She's not usually so short with our customers. She had a rough night, and to make matters worse, her tire blew out this morning. Walt's helping her to get it replaced."

Kade liked April. Liked her husband, Seth, too. The man had done a damn fine job of helping him build his new motel. The work was ahead of schedule, and if things continued as they had, he'd have the place opened before the holidays.

Speaking of someone to help her, where the hell was her boyfriend? "Why is her car still sitting on Walt's truck? If she wants, I can help her change the tire, no charge."

"That's probably not a good idea," Kimber offered. "If I were you, I'd let Walt handle it."

He furrowed his brows, sensing a deeper story. "Why's that? Is she above neighborly help?"

April and Kimber shared a look before April focused on him. "Her boyfriend broke up with her last night, and she's feeling... shall we say, a little raw right now where guys are concerned. Walt's safe territory. You're not."

He snorted, totally understanding. In fact, he'd been in a similar situation not all that long ago with his ex-wife. He opened his wallet and removed enough cash to pay for his coffee, plus a nice tip. "I see. She's wounded and likely to lash out. I'll keep my distance for a while."

When he caught sight of the bright yellow flier taped to the front door, he pointed toward it. "She should sign up for the continuing education auto maintenance class. The instructor will teach her how to change a tire, change the oil, along with other stuff a single lady should know."

Both women studied him with surprised gazes.

"That's a great idea," Kimber said. "You seem to know women pretty well."

He laughed. "I should. I have five sisters."

April widened her eyes as if he'd shocked her. "*Five*? Are you still sane?"

He grinned. "I am now. Growing up? It was rough at times. But they're great teachers. They made sure I knew exactly how to treat a lady."

"Dang," Kimber said, elbowing April. "It's too bad we're already married."

"Right?" April said with a big smile.

He shook his head, enjoying the ladies' flirtations. "Talk like that will go to a man's head."

April widened her eyes, giving him a false-innocent look while Kimber busted out with a laugh.

He'd expect that kind of innuendo from the guys, but not these ladies, and he chuckled. "I walked right into that one, didn't I?"

Kimber shrugged and smiled.

Yes, he would like it here in Aspen. "Okay. I'd better head back to work. Thank you for the coffee and the laughs. April? When you and Noelle have a spare moment, I'd like to talk to you about possibly providing a light continental breakfast for my guests if you're interested. I believe it would be a mutually beneficial relationship."

She nodded happily. "I think that's a wonderful idea. We were hoping your guests would stop over for breakfast, but this sounds like a much better option. I'll hit up Noelle when she's in a better mood and get back to you."

He lifted his coffee cup in a toast. "Let me know when you do. Have a good morning."

Noelle looked at him as he left the building. He smiled once again, but she only stared.

"Morning, Walt. Miss Parker," he said in greeting before he headed back to help with the tile installation.

All in all, he'd had a brilliant morning.

———

With April's blessing, Noelle left Rumors early the following Tuesday evening and drove to the small high school on the outskirts of Aspen. Class sizes in Aspen were tiny compared to what she'd endured growing up, and Noelle was envious of the tight-knit community it offered. She'd attended four high schools during the years she'd been passed from one foster family to the next. The smallest had been almost ten times the size of Aspen's high school.

She'd been a lost girl, lost in the crowd of kids.

Thank God she'd found her home in Aspen.

She pulled to the back of the building according to the class instructions and parked next to the open auto-shop bay. She had to admit she was nervous about taking on a new challenge, but the thought of not having to rely on anyone for car issues left her empowered.

Late afternoon heat radiated off the blacktop, and she was glad she'd changed into old cutoffs and a light t-shirt before she'd left work. She doubted they'd have air-conditioning in the building, and the temps had hit eighty-five that day. The nights had grown cooler, but the days could still sizzle.

The inside of the building was a dark contrast to the bright blue sky hovering overhead. Scents of gas and grease permeated the air like a mysterious perfume that enticed her into a stranger's lair. She thought she'd hate the smell, but it was masculine and kind of sexy.

She took a few moments to blink as she adjusted to the change in light before she spotted six folding chairs placed off to the side of the open bay. Two other classmates sat, waiting, including Betty Johnson, the sixty-something owner of Johnson Realty.

Noelle walked toward her, secretively eyeing the cute brunette sitting in the back row. She'd always wished she'd been born with darker hair. The woman and Betty both had on jeans, and Noelle wondered if she'd focused more on the heat of the day instead of functionality.

Leave it to her to be the odd one in class.

"Hi," said the brunette as Noelle approached.

The friendliness in the woman's gaze coaxed a smile from her. "Hi."

She took the seat next to Betty in the front row and glanced around, feeling intimidated by the various tools and work-stations.

The brunette leaned forward. "My name's Krystal."

Betty and Noelle both introduced themselves before Nancy Sykes, a slender, blond woman near Betty's age, joined the crowd. If Betty and Nancy could take on this challenge at their ages, she certainly could.

Nancy sat next to Krystal, and Betty turned to talk to her. "Nancy. It's good to see you. Rumor is you're dating Wayne Staker. Is that true?"

Nancy blushed. "Who told you that?"

The realtor grinned. "I saw Milo and Anna at the grocery store the other day. Her baby bump is pretty darn cute."

That brightened Nancy's expression. "I know. I'm so excited to be a grandma."

Noelle smiled. She'd heard talk that Anna was pregnant. It was nice to see two people in love building a family.

"You didn't answer my question," Betty whispered to Nancy.

"Welcome," said a deep voice as their instructor approached from behind, saving Nancy from responding.

Noelle looked over her shoulder to see who'd be teaching them and gaped. The moisture in her mouth evaporated as Kade Collier strode to the front of the chairs. She caught a whiff of his sexy cologne before he came to a stop no more than six feet in front of her, causing her to tilt her head back to see him.

"No," she said beneath her breath.

Betty leaned close. "Did you say something, dear?"

She shook her head as she stared at Kade.

He glanced over the class, not looking at her any longer than he did the rest of his students. In fact, he didn't seem surprised to see her there, nor affected in any sort of way.

She was stunned, to say the least. She considered walking out, but then that would leave her the topic of discussion amongst the residents of Aspen, and she'd already heard several whispers about her and Ian breaking up in her own coffee shop that day.

Kade smiled, a slight dimple showing in his right cheek. "Thank you all for signing up for this class." "As you know, Aspen's trying to generate additional revenue for the school, while also providing valuable educational opportunities for its residents. Besides signing up for classes, you can help by spreading the word to your friends."

He paused to give each of them a friendly smile. "This is a six-week class during which we'll cover the basics of auto mechanics. You don't need any special skills or tools, just the desire to learn. My name is Kade Collier, and I see a couple of familiar faces in the group."

Noelle glanced at the rest of them, wondering who, besides her, knew him.

"I grew up in Pinecone," he continued. "But I moved away for a while before coming home. I'm the proprietor of the Hidden Springs Motel in Pinecone, and my latest motel is under construction next door to Miss Parker's coffee shop. I volunteered to teach this class as a way to get to know the good people of Aspen."

Betty and Nancy smiled and nodded, while Krystal stared at Kade with complete adoration. Disbelief rolled through Noelle. Not only would she have to sit through six classes with Kade as her teacher, but she'd have to endure them with his groupie fawning over him as well.

Certainly, she could concoct a decent enough excuse to miss class next time.

Kade cleared his throat. "Some of you may wonder why a motel owner is teaching an auto mechanics class. Truth is, classic cars are a passion of mine. In fact, I'm happy to see Miss Parker here. I've had my eye on her '67 Mustang for a while now, and I'd love to get a peek beneath her hood."

Everyone in the class turned to her.

Heat coursed up Noelle's cheeks. It didn't help that he kept calling her by her formal name, either. "Please. My name is Noelle."

He met her gaze, giving her a warm smile that somehow declared victory while pulling her in at the same time. "Noelle."

That was the second time he'd said it to her—once the other day in the coffee shop—and both times the way he said her name left her with a shiver.

She blinked to break the spell he seemed to have cast over her. "Will you be teaching us how to change a tire?" That's all she really needed to know. Not how brown his eyes were. Not how much she wished her pillow smelled like him.

Correction. Not him. Just his cologne.

A spark flashed in his eyes. "That and so much more if you hang around long enough."

———

Kade turned away from the class to hide his enjoyment. He'd purposefully pushed Noelle's buttons, drew her out into the open, unwilling to let her hide even amongst the small group. He wanted to flirt with her, spar with her, and do anything to chase away the sadness he'd discovered in her eyes days earlier.

Unfortunately, he recognized the pain simmering beneath her forced smile, and he hated to see others suffer as he had. If he could help brighten her day, give her something else to think about, he'd do it.

Someone had once done the same for him, and he intended to pay it forward.

4

Noelle studied Kade as he stood in front of the class, lecturing them. As much as she wanted to be annoyed by him, she was more than a little interested in the topic.

Kade glanced at the paper he held before he continued speaking in his deep, smooth voice. "One of the easiest things you can do to maintain your car is to check your tire pressure. Properly inflated tires handle better, and your tires will last longer, not to mention you'll get better gas mileage. Under-inflated tires are also the leading cause of most blowouts. I realize the computers on some cars will read this for you, but it can't hurt to learn how to check, anyway."

Noelle knew all about that joyous experience, and she inwardly groaned.

Kade glanced at the group. "How many of you carry a tire pressure gauge in your car?"

Noelle watched everyone raise a hand but her. Feeling incompetent, she dropped her gaze to the cement floor beneath her feet and studied a crack.

"Noelle?"

She flicked her gaze to him in a blink.

Kade lifted his chin. "Do you have a tire gauge?"

She wouldn't know if she did. "What does it look like?"

Her response brought a smile to his face. He lifted a slender, silver device that looked much like a pen.

She shook her head. She'd always had Walt check her tires for her. When she remembered. For all she knew, she'd probably driven down the road with under-inflated tires for most of her life.

He approached and handed the one in his hand to her, his eyes snaring hers for an uncomfortable few seconds. "It just so happens I have an extra."

She wrapped her fingers around the cool silver metal and gave him the briefest of smiles. "Thanks."

He dipped his head and kept speaking. "Enough talking. Let's move our chairs out of the way, and I'll have each of you move your cars into a stall. We'll practice checking tire pressures, and then we'll move into changing a tire since that's a skill Noelle desires."

That's what she desired? She gave a mental snort. What she desired was a gorgeous, sweet man with a million dollars who would love and take care of her for the rest of her days. And change her tires for her.

However, the millionaire hottie wasn't an option at the moment, so she'd do what she needed to take care of herself.

She pulled her keys from her pocket and headed out into the bright sunlight, sensing Kade's gaze on her. She set the tire gauge on the seat next to her as she started her car. It seemed he'd constantly singled her out. But was that because she was the least experienced in auto mechanics?

There was an obvious attraction on his part. Maybe. Something, anyway. When she'd seen him in town, she was certain he'd flirted with her. But in class, he seemed to be pretty friendly with all the ladies.

The entire strange interaction left her off-balance.

She shifted her car into gear, grateful to have a new tire to check, and drove toward the bay. Kade stood near the entrance and waved her inside. She followed his directions and tried not to notice the mischief sparkling in his eyes each time he smiled at her.

What was up with him? She wanted to be annoyed, but there was something warm and engaging about him, too.

Once everyone was inside, he motioned the group toward Krystal's car. When they'd gathered, he spoke again. "The place you want to look to find the correct tire pressure for your vehicle is inside the driver's side door, along this edge."

He pointed to the correct spot. "It says Krystal's proper tire pressure is thirty-five. Krystal? Why don't you come here and give it a shot?"

Krystal smiled as she stepped forward, obviously happy to have the teacher's attention.

If Noelle had to guess, she'd say she was a few years younger than her. Thick, dark curls cascaded down her back and over one shoulder, and her snug gray t-shirt showed off her trim waist and well-endowed breasts.

What guy wouldn't be attracted to that?

Krystal crouched next to Kade, her tire gauge in hand.

"A couple of things to note," he said, smiling at Krystal before looking at the class. "The thing sticking out of your tire is called a valve stem, and the cap on the end is a valve cap, okay? You'll want to take off the valve cap to check the pressure."

The class watched while Krystal removed the valve cap on her tire. She pressed the rounded end of the gauge over the valve stem, and the tire responded with a hiss.

Kade squatted next to Krystal, and Noelle suddenly wished

he'd singled her out again that time. "All you need is a second or two to get the correct reading," he said.

He took the gauge from the pretty brunette and read the pressure. "Thirty-five. This tire is properly inflated. You can all go ahead and check your tires now. I'll be around in case you have questions and to check your technique. The shop also has an air pump if any of your tires are low."

Noelle walked to her car and opened the driver's side door. As annoying as Kade could be, this was good information to have. She'd have to thank April and Kimber for pushing her in this direction.

She found the sticker with her correct tire pressure and moved to the first tire. Squatting down, she removed the valve cap and promptly dropped it. Groaning, she captured it before it could roll away. Then, feeling awkward, she placed the rounded end over the valve stem like Kade had shown them and pressed. The white marker popped out of the bottom of the gauge and stopped at the little five marking.

She frowned. That couldn't be right. Walt had checked all her tires when he'd mounted her new one. Her car should be in top shape.

She made another attempt, and the gauge wobbled in her hands as she tried to put it on correctly. The valve hissed again, giving her a reading of almost ten that time.

"You need to get it on straight and solid."

Noelle startled, not realizing Kade had come up behind her. "How?" Her frustration came through in the tone of her voice.

He reacted by smiling. "Let me show you."

He knelt next to her, and an unwanted shiver raced over her skin. It aggravated her to be so hyper aware of him, and she hated that her body responded to his presence.

His hand grazed hers as he took the gauge. "Hold this over the end until it feels stable and then press it straight on." He completed the action, and the white marker shot outward. "Thirty-five p.s.i. Perfect."

"It should be," she murmured. Her new tire had cost her more than she'd been prepared to spend that month.

"Go ahead and replace the valve cap."

Of course her fingers shook as she did.

He stood and held out a hand to her. "Let's do the next one."

She didn't want to accept his offer, but she'd appear rude if she didn't. Then he'd wonder why, and he'd discover he affected her, and she wanted him to believe he meant nothing to her at all.

Which he didn't.

She slid her fingers across his warm palm and sucked in a quiet breath. He gripped her wrist and tugged her to her feet. The electrical current his touch created zipped through her, leaving her pulse racing. "Thank you," she whispered.

He caught her gaze before he released her hand. "My pleasure."

Noelle swallowed, wishing she could turn and run. If life would allow her, she'd hide in a cave where no attractive men could ever tempt her.

She slipped from his grasp and moved to the other side of her car. Without waiting for direction, she lowered to the ground, twisted off the valve cap, and checked the pressure. This time, the gauge worked, giving her the proper tire pressure.

Noelle glanced up to find him staring at her. Not at her face, though. He had his gaze trained straight down her t-shirt. The moment he realized that she'd moved, he switched his focus to her face.

Interest burned in his molten chocolate eyes and shot straight to her core.

Oh no. No, no, no, no, *no*.

She would not fall for another attractive guy who'd break her heart.

She stood and met his gaze dead on, forcing hers to be the polar opposite of his. Cool and disinterested. "I think I've got it. I'm sure someone else could use your help."

He stared at her for a moment, and then a smile broke over his face. "Yep. You did great. Why don't you practice by testing your others, and I'll check on Krystal and Betty?"

You do that, she thought as he walked away. Let him hit on Krystal. Or Betty, for that matter. Perhaps their hearts were in better shape and could chance another hit.

Once he was out of range, she let loose a sigh and watched him saunter toward Krystal. He said something, and Krystal laughed. Then she stood and pushed him playfully in the chest.

Jealousy reared its head, and Noelle squashed it like a spider crawling across her bed. She absolutely had done the right thing by not encouraging his interest.

Kade and Krystal talked for a moment more, and then they both switched their gazes to Noelle. Heated awkwardness warmed her cheeks, and she squatted to check another tire.

What could they possibly have said about her?

———

For Noelle, learning to change a tire was a completely different story. If checking air pressure was a walk in the park, learning how to change a tire was an exhausting marathon. Kade had gone through the steps with the class multiple times before allowing them to attempt it. Noelle had watched each of the other ladies practice setting their jacks and lifting their cars. With a little help from Kaden, they'd removed their tires before replacing them and tightened the lug nuts.

They'd been in class long enough for the sun to set, leaving the outside dark beyond the bay doors. Betty and Nancy had practiced first because Betty needed to get home to her husband and Nancy had a date.

Krystal finished turning the tire iron on her last lug nut before she stepped back to let Kade check her work. He put the wrench on each of the lug nuts and tested them. Then he stood with a smile. "Good job, little sister."

Sister?

Krystal beamed and slapped her palms together to wipe off whatever grime she'd encountered. "I told you I could do it. Everyone always says I'm such a princess, but I can get my hands dirty when I need to."

"Yeah?" Kade answered, tossing a rag for her hands. "Then how about the next time Dad needs help in the barn, you step up?"

She laughed and shook her head. "I don't think so. That's your job. And if you tell Mom or Dad what I'm doing here, I'll tell them about the time you came home stupid drunk, left the gate open, and let the horses out."

"Geez, Krystal. That was almost ten years ago." He flicked a glance at Noelle, probably to see her reaction, but she remained expressionless.

Krystal gave him a sassy grin. "Doesn't matter. It'll still damage your perfect reputation."

He snorted. "I'm hardly perfect."

"Don't I know?" She smiled at Noelle. "I'm going to head out, too. I have to drive back to Pinecone tonight, and I have a class in the morning."

Noelle had often wondered if she should take some online classes, but she had no idea what kind of degree she'd want. "What are you studying?"

"Nursing. I'll have my degree in December. Thank God," she added, rolling her eyes.

"Congratulations," Noelle said. "That's impressive."

Krystal shrugged. "It's something I love."

Kade slid his gaze to her. "Kind of like you with your coffee shop,"

She nodded. Although coffee *was* her passion, Kade couldn't know that.

"So, I'm out of here." Krystal gave Kade a quick hug. "Nice to meet you, Noelle."

"You, too," she said and then watched the only person who kept things this side of awkward get into her car and back out the bay door.

They both stood watching Krystal's car until her taillights were a memory.

Kade turned to her. "Okay. Your turn."

5

Noelle's nerves twisted and tightened as she approached her car. She'd watched the other three women change a tire. Which meant she should know what to do, but suddenly her mind wouldn't focus on anything but the attractive man following behind her.

Baby steps, she reminded herself. Just do one thing at a time.

First, she went to her trunk and opened it. Her new spare tire, tire iron, and jack waited for her. All in all, they appeared to be powerful adversaries that seemed difficult to conquer.

She'd start with the tire iron.

Kade walked past her, drawing his finger along the side of her car with the tenderness of a lover. "I've always thought a '67 Mustang had beautiful lines."

She dropped the tire iron next to the tire she intended to remove and returned for the jack. "Me, too. Unfortunately, I didn't realize how much upkeep an older car requires."

Kade lifted his brows and looked at her. Once again, the overwhelming depths of his beautiful eyes hit her. "That's the beauty of it, though. Tinkering under the hood until she purrs. Waxing her paint until she shines."

Sexy, passionate words about something he obviously loved, but she didn't miss the flirtation underneath. "That's some pretty poetry right there."

He shrugged. "I call it how I see it. If you don't want her, I'd be happy to take her off your hands."

Noelle glanced at her car. As much of a pain as she'd been lately, she couldn't part with her. "No. Now that I've had a convertible, I can't go back."

Kade softly snorted. "You enjoy going topless, huh?"

She widened her eyes at the innuendo. "Why does it always have to be about sex?"

It was his turn to lift his brows. "Excuse me?"

"Tinkering under the hood until she purrs? Going topless? Can guys use their brains for once instead?"

He studied her for a moment, the air brilliantly tense. "I'm sorry if I offended you. Yes, I sometimes compare women to cars, but only because I admire both. That doesn't mean I make everything about sex."

Uncomfortable heat singed her cheeks. She'd been too blunt. But she wasn't wrong. Frustrated, she waved away his apology with a flick of her hand. "It's not just you. It's all guys. Nothing seems to matter besides sex."

Kade cleared his throat. "First, you can't lump all guys together any more than I can say all girls tease guys until we're out of our minds and then dump us."

The validity of what he said smacked her. She was in a vulnerable, raw spot, and she needed to keep her biased judgments to herself. She folded her arms. "I'm sorry. I shouldn't have said anything. My head's not in the right place, and you certainly don't need to hear my crazy thoughts."

He tilted his head, eyeing her. "Except you still believe them."

She gaped, knowing he'd pegged her and wouldn't let her off the hook. She tried to think of another way to extricate herself, but none came.

A hint of a smile crossed his lips. "Second, yes. Lots of things matter to me besides sex. I can't say I don't enjoy it, any more than I can say I don't enjoy a beautiful car." He gave her Mustang another caress. "But I'm not that shallow, Noelle."

She wasn't sure she could believe him. "It's not the same. Guys can have sex and not form a relationship. Girls have a harder time. So, guys use us and then discard us when the next sweet thing comes along."

Kade slowly shook his head. "Again, another generalization."

He was right, but he didn't understand her point. "But your hearts don't break the same. Sometimes, they don't break at all."

The warmth in his eyes chilled. "You're wrong about that."

She wanted to continue to argue, but something in his gaze stopped her. He *had* experienced pain. She could see that clearly.

She blinked and looked down, ashamed of what she'd thrown at him. "I'm sorry. I recently broke up with someone," she said with a forced laugh. "In case you can't tell. I've taken it out on you, and I sincerely apologize. When you started flirting with me—"

Kade narrowed his eyes in dispute. "Flirting?"

His mock innocence drew a smile to her face. "Yes, flirting. Don't deny it."

He tilted his head and gave her the barest nod of acknowledgement. "Fine. I might have flirted. But barely."

She snorted. "Oh, more than barely. You can't deny what

you said, and I caught you checking me out when I was testing my tire pressure."

He straightened, giving her a look that sent her pulse racing. "Okay. I'm guilty. But what do you expect? You're a beautiful woman. Even if I could ignore you, I couldn't ignore your car."

She stared up at him, finding herself backed into a nice corner. She'd forced him to admit he was attracted to her, and she now didn't know how to respond. "Well."

He dropped his gaze, looking at her from face to foot and then back up again. "Well? That's all you have to say?"

She nodded. "I should change this tire."

He laughed, the sound echoing through the quiet building. "Okay, then. I guess you'd better get to it."

He hovered while she set up the jack. When she squatted in order to slip the jack beneath her car, he stopped her. "Wait a second."

She sat on the cement and watched as he walked to his shiny silver truck and opened the door. He returned a moment later, carrying a dark gray button-down shirt, and held it out to her. "Put this on. If you lay on the ground in that white shirt, it'll never come clean. And next time, read the class disclosure more carefully. It says to wear comfortable clothing that can get dirty."

She took the shirt from him and didn't argue. "Thank you."

As she slipped her arms inside the sleeves, his scent reached up to taunt her. She inhaled carefully so he wouldn't notice as she rolled up the long sleeves.

She thanked him again as she curled onto her shoulder and then on to her back, slipping her head beneath the car like the others had done. The underneath of her Mustang was a foreign, intriguing place. "What am I looking for?"

"A flat metal surface. Once you find it, start turning the jack handle until it's almost raised and then place it in the proper position."

She searched the bottom of her car and was surprised when he laid down beside her. Excitement shot through her, and she battled it into submission. The garage had suddenly become far too intimate.

He reached across her and pointed to a metal bar. "There's a good spot."

She scooted out and sat up to grab the jack and begin twisting the handle. As she did, she continually glanced at the lower, exposed portion of the man next to her. As hard as she tried to focus on the jack, her gaze drifted to the dark t-shirt that stretched across his abs and then lower.

"Got it?" he asked.

She startled. "I think so."

Enough with the gawking. She lowered herself to the ground again and bumped his shoulder as she settled next to him and wedged the jack into place. The tight space beneath the car made moving awkward, but she managed to crank the handle until the jack sat squarely beneath the bar.

He nudged her with an elbow. "Okay. Let's get out of the way before you lift it."

She slid out and sat up, then got to her knees, the cement floor hard beneath her.

Kade lifted his chin. "Did you put the brick in place to keep the car from rolling?"

She groaned and climbed to her feet, disappointed that she was already making mistakes. She found the brick where Krystal had left it and returned to wedge it behind the back tire.

"Don't forget that part," he cautioned. "You can use a brick or a rock, but use something. You don't want the car to roll and fall off the jack."

"Right." She nodded and returned to cranking the jack. Inch

by inch, her car lifted off the ground until her tire was no longer touching the cement.

"Good job," he said. "Now loosen each of the lug nuts in turn."

She put the wrench on the first lug nut and tried to turn it, but it wouldn't budge. "It's stuck."

"You might have to put your body weight into it. Give it some muscle."

She inhaled and then groaned as she gave it everything she had. She ended up standing and pushing downward before it budged.

Kade sighed. "Shops are supposed to hand-tighten the lug nuts the last bit so they're not too difficult, but a lot of times they don't bother. I'll mention it to Walt next time I see him. Especially for the ladies."

She focused on her work until she had all the lug nuts off. Then she jerked on the tire and wiggled it until she had it on the ground. She was breathless from the exertion, but damn proud of herself. "*I did it.*"

He laughed. "Yes, you did. Now you can put it back on."

She narrowed her gaze and shook her head. "Killjoy."

He only grinned in response.

Noelle set to work putting her car back together. When she finished, she smiled at him, now understanding the elation on the others' faces when they'd done the same. With a smug smile, she handed the tire wrench to him. "Check it."

He placed it over a lug nut and tightened it, the muscles in his arms flexing as he did.

"*Hey.* Don't make them too tight." She might have to take them off again.

"They must be on good and snug, sweetheart. We don't want them to fall off while you're driving down the road."

She tensed at the word, *sweetheart*. Then decided he probably said that to a lot of ladies, and she shouldn't take it person-ally. She certainly didn't want a repeat of their earlier conversation.

He finished and then nodded to her. "Go ahead and release the jack. You, my dear, are good to go."

She tucked in her bottom lip to hold back a grin.

"Thank you for this," she said as she placed the jack in her trunk. "I don't know if you realize how empowering this is to women."

He snorted. "I have five sisters. If you count my mom, that's six women I help. The more they can do for themselves, the better."

She was certain he was the kind of man who would do that for them. "Right. I'm sure you make them change their own tires."

He shrugged. "Well."

She wished she had even one sibling, someone who belonged to her no matter what. "It sounds like you have a great family. I hope you count yourself lucky."

"Eh. I can take 'em or leave 'em." But he followed that with a grin. "Just kidding. My family's great."

She sighed and nodded. Of course, they were. He probably had no idea what it was like to be truly alone.

"You?" he asked.

She lifted a shoulder and let it drop. "Orphan."

He seemed genuinely surprised. "Seriously?"

Most people were. "Seriously."

She wasn't sure if compassion or pity flickered in his gaze. Whichever it was, she didn't want either of them. "It happens."

She glanced toward her car and then back at him. "I should go. It's late. Thank you for everything."

"My pleasure," he said. "Will you be back next week?"

He'd asked as though he wasn't certain, which she found

slightly endearing. "Of course. You're teaching important things I need to learn."

He smiled and nodded. "Good. I'll see you then. If not sooner. It's hard to pass up your coffee."

Attraction twisted through her, strong and sweet, and she cursed herself for feeling it. She turned and opened her car door, intending to leave before she started flirting back.

He was at her side before she could close it.

She looked up at him, not sure what to say.

He gave her a nod. "Drive carefully. Don't freak out if you see me following you. I want to make sure you make it back to Aspen with no trouble."

She swallowed. "Okay." What else could she say? He was only being a gentleman, and she appreciated it immensely.

He helped her back out of the bay, and she turned and headed toward town. She was certain he wouldn't catch up to her, since he still needed to close the shop and get into his truck.

Despite her doubts, she hadn't been driving for more than a few minutes when his truck lights bore down on her. He had to be going at least ten over the speed limit to catch her.

When she approached the turn to her lane, she rolled down her window and waved her thanks. He continued past, leaving her with shivers of excitement. And anxiety.

It wasn't until she'd parked her car and headed into her house that she realized she still wore his shirt. She shrugged out of it and tossed it on the back of her couch, thinking she could give it back the next time they had class, if not sooner.

Then she paused, picked it up again, and brought it to her nose. Hints of oil and grease clung to it, but she mostly smelled the same cologne he'd worn during class.

And it smelled good.

Damn good.

6

Noelle parked in her regular spot near Rumors the next morning, happy to see Kade's truck in front of his own building. He'd disturbed her dreams the previous night, but she was determined he wouldn't disturb her days.

He could be a great friend, she'd decided. Besides, it was better to be friendly with the neighboring business owners than enemies. After all, they were all citizens of Aspen, trying to make a good life and a decent living. They needed to support each other. She supposed she could forgive him for plowing down the field of wildflowers next to her shop, too.

When she stepped out of her car, she spotted him instantly. He was out front again, like he'd been the other morning, and he watched her like he had then. She lifted a hand and waved.

He did the same. He said something to the worker who stood with him and then headed in her direction.

"Oh hell," she whispered. She didn't want him to walk over and talk to her. She'd thought about him nearly every second since she'd left the previous night, and no one needed to tell her she stood at the head of a dangerous road. In a desperate need to avoid him, she quickened her pace, but he was at her door before she had it unlocked.

"Good morning," Kade said. The familiar charming smile curved his lips and tugged at her heart. "I hope you don't mind, but I wanted to ask your opinion."

She finished unlocking her door and then glanced up at him with questioning brows. He wore a ball cap over his dark hair, and the interested look in his brown eyes whispered to her heart.

He gestured toward the inside of her shop. "Don't let me make you late. The guys won't forgive me if I delay their coffee. I can talk while you work."

He'd given her no choice. She started to open the door, but he grabbed it and held it for her instead. She sucked in a fortifying breath and stepped inside.

The quiet morning greeted her like it always did, but this time a current of intense energy raced along with the silence. She flipped on the lights and glanced his way again, wishing he'd ask his question and leave.

He studied her eyes, further increasing her attraction to him. In a defensive move, she turned and walked behind the counter, placing the precious barrier between them. "What can I help you with?"

He leaned against the counter as though he had no idea how he affected her. "I thought about you last night, about our class, I mean. I had some ideas planned for the next couple of classes, but I thought I'd pick your brain. What other things do ladies need to know?"

"Um…" She pulled an apron from behind the counter and tied it around her. One more barrier to protect her. "In the past, I've had problems with my battery and changing windshield wipers."

"Okay, good. How about changing your air filter and changing the oil?"

She slipped the band from around her wrist and pulled back her hair. He studied her every move, making her more nervous. "Changing the oil seems a little intimidating. I'm not sure I can do it."

"Sure, you can. With instructions and the right tools." He glanced around her shop. "I'd compare it to teaching someone how to make muffins or bread."

She laughed then. "Are you kidding? Those things are easy."

"Because you've learned them." He held her with his intense gaze, sending her emotions fluttering.

"Are you asking me to teach you to make bread?" The instant she spoke, she regretted it.

"Are you offering?" His grin returned. "It might be interesting."

She blinked and looked away, forcing a laugh. "It certainly might."

"So?" he pressed.

"Maybe we should focus on car stuff first." Those classes would take place in a public building with other students. Much safer.

"Okay, then. But when you're an automotive pro, I might hit you up again."

She smiled and nodded. "You're persistent, if nothing else."

He didn't hesitate to nod. "It pays to be in my line of business."

"Motel owner?"

He grinned. "Not just. I'm an entrepreneur."

She lifted her brows in amusement. "Entrepreneur?"

Then she realized Kade's unassuming manner had snuck right past her defenses. She tried to resurrect them, but as long as he had his decadent brown eyes trained on her, she couldn't. "What else do you do besides own small-town motels?"

Happiness flashed in his eyes. "It's a secret."

She laughed then. "A secret?"

He nodded. "I might tell you later. After I've had my morning coffee."

Except she'd figured him out. "I see. You don't really have secrets. You only want coffee."

He studied her with an engaging expression. "No. I have some seriously amazing secrets. But if I told everyone, they wouldn't be secrets."

She grinned. "Now, I'm *everyone*?"

He stopped and held her gaze. "No. You're definitely one of a kind."

The jovial air around them deepened, setting off her alarms. She searched for an excuse so he'd leave, but he saved her the trouble when he gestured toward the door with a tilt of his head. "I should go. I only meant to say good morning and ask your opinion. See you in class."

She was about to ask if he'd be back for coffee, but she bit her tongue instead.

Let him go. *Let him go.*

———

Kade's boots crunched on the gravel as he made his way back to his motel property, feeling damn good. The old saying about the giver getting more than the receiver might be true. He'd been trying to brighten Noelle's morning. Facing a new dawn could be tough. But making her smile had lit something bright and warm in his heart.

A gorgeous September sun warmed the crisp morning air, leaving the day fresh with possibilities. His motel would be open before the holidays. Interest rates had allowed him to add more units than he'd originally thought, and he'd made genuine tracks with the townspeople. With each passing day, Aspen became more and more his new home.

He stepped inside the nearly finished building and eyed the rustic furnishings that the crew continued to add each day. The major portion of his business would come from fly-fishermen looking for an escape, but as the town grew and expanded, more and more people would stop by. He had yet to locate a good fishing guide to partner with, but that was next on his list.

Damn. He'd forgotten to ask Noelle about the idea he'd proposed to April.

Though he now had another reason to stop by later. Maybe he'd sneak over at lunch for soup and a sandwich. Another logical reason to see Noelle without seeming like he chased her.

———

Every cup of coffee Noelle had poured that morning reminded her of the color of Kade's dark eyes. Which reminded her of his charming smile. Which sent her nerves into a tangled mass.

She needed to stop.

She could see, as plain as black and white, that she stood on the same path to heartbreak as she had with Ian and Tyler. When they'd shown the slightest interest, she'd bitten like a rainbow trout on a worm, using no intelligence whatsoever.

Just because a guy smiled or flirted did not mean she needed to react or open her heart.

She knew this. Knew she had to keep her resolve where Kade was concerned. At least until he'd proven himself.

The bell on the front door chimed, and she jerked her head to see who'd entered. Then cursed again and started over at square one with her mental reprimands as April walked in and made her way toward the counter. Today was April's late day because she'd volunteered at her son's preschool class, and left there to show up at Rumors right before the lunch crowd.

"How did the auto class go last night?" April asked as she donned an apron.

"It was great. Definitely worth the money. Next time you get a flat, don't hesitate to call me. Better yet, you should join the class. I'm sure Kade would catch you up on what we learned last night."

"Kade?" April's puzzled gaze turned into a smile. "Is he the teacher?"

Aspen was a small town, and things like that happened. "Yeah. Trust me. I was as surprised as you are. A weird coincidence, don't you think?"

"Or not. Noelle, he was the one who suggested to me and Kimber that you sign up." She laughed. "I think he's kind of into you."

The contents of her stomach turned sour. "No." She didn't want to believe it, didn't want it to be true.

April shrugged. "Why fight it? He's cute. And he's ambitious. Seems like a good catch."

She placed a hand on her hip. "If I was *fishing*. Which I'm not. I'm not ready to date again, April. Not sure when I will be." Or *if* she would be.

Noelle headed for the backroom to stir the pot of chili she'd thrown together for the day's soup. April followed her and washed her hands before she lifted the pan of breadsticks from the counter and placed them in the oven.

"Maybe you need a hair of the dog that bit you," April said as she moved to grab a second pan.

Noelle snorted. "That's for a hangover, not dating."

"You sort of have a dating hangover. Don't you think? Too much of the wrong thing and now you have a headache?"

Headache? Heartache? What difference did it make? She didn't answer as she stirred the chili with a large wooden spoon.

"He seems like a nice guy," April continued. "Maybe you should give him a chance."

"I don't think so."

The front chimes rang again, and she glanced at April. "I'll get it."

Noelle wiped her hands as she returned to the front area, and her heart flipped when she found Kade waiting at the counter. *Damn it.*

"Hi," she said tentatively. She hadn't expected to see him in her shop twice on the same day.

He gave her a sheepish grin that totally tugged at her heart. "You're probably wondering why I'm back."

She returned his smile and gave him a noncommittal shrug of her shoulders.

"Two things. First, I'd like a bowl of that delicious-smelling chili, and second, I meant to ask you earlier about a partnership with Rumors to provide a continental breakfast for the motel. I'd mentioned it to April, but I wanted to talk to you, too." He glanced around the empty room. "Do you have a moment?"

7

Noelle stared into Kade's eyes. The same eyes that had haunted her all morning. "I'm kind of busy right now. The lunch crowd will be here soon."

"It's okay," April said from behind her. "I'll cover it. If it gets too crazy, I'll let you know."

Noelle shot her a peeved look that Kade couldn't see. April returned with a bright, far too helpful smile.

She turned back to Kade. "If it won't take long."

"I'll bring your soup," April called to Kade. "It's on the house since you're discussing business."

He lifted a hand. "That's very nice, but unnecessary. I'm happy to pay."

April waved away his reply. "We're happy to have you here, so make yourself comfortable."

Noelle would seriously wring her neck at the first opportunity. "We can sit over here." She led him to the table closest to the counter, where it seemed the safest. As soon as more than one customer walked in, she'd make her excuses.

Until then, she released a nervous breath and took a seat. He sat opposite her and placed a yellow legal pad on the small café table between them. When she'd designed the space in her shop, she'd thought the close seating would be perfect for all customers. Now she knew otherwise.

He flipped a couple of pages on his pad. "Let me fill you in on my expected needs, and you can let me know what you think."

She nodded.

He captured her gaze and held it, studying her for a few extra seconds that sent her nerves tingling. Then he released her from his potent stare and checked his notes. "Coffee for sure. Muffins. Fruit if you're ordering it for your shop. And maybe whatever your breakfast special is for the day. How soon, in advance, would I need to place our order?"

She blinked and tried to focus on business. "Thanks for thinking of us. This will definitely increase our revenue."

"Are you kidding? Your food might be what makes my motel the place of choice between here and Pinecone. Besides, I like it when I can help others. Helping you also helps me."

She liked that about him, liked that he seemed to consider others such as his sisters, or that he'd made sure she'd found her way home safely. She gestured to him with open palms. "As far as ordering, we can be flexible with numbers, but we'd need to have a definite count two days in advance. We can bring over extra coffee anytime you run out. I'd suggest two carafes each of regular and decaf to start the morning. I'd recommend ordering an extra dozen muffins each day, and the number of guests plus two to three extra servings of the special. Unless they're serving themselves. Then maybe one and a half times your guests."

She stopped talking when she found him staring at her. "Is there a problem?"

He grinned. "Nope. I always tell my sisters there's nothing sexier than a smart woman."

A warm blush heated her cheeks. She'd never considered

herself overly intelligent, but she supposed she knew a fair amount about the coffee shop business. "Could we stick to business?" she said, but she couldn't keep a smile from curving her lips.

His engaging eyes sparkled as he leaned back in his chair, extending his muscular legs next to her. "Absolutely."

As if she could focus now. "I'd have to work on the numbers, but we could probably extend a ten percent discount since you'll be a guaranteed regular customer. If you want, I can work up a proposal and bring it over later."

He hit her with a charming smile. "Maybe we could talk over dinner? I know a great place in Pinecone."

Her heart screamed for her to answer yes. "I don't think that's a good idea."

His smile grew bigger. "I'm inclined to disagree, but I'll let you have your way." He paused for a second. "This time."

Something tender and tight twisted inside her. "So, I'll bring the proposal over later."

"Around six?"

She nodded. "That'll be perfect. That's right when I get off work."

"I know." He nodded toward the kitchen. "Do you think I could get that chili to go? I should probably get back to the worksite."

She stood, feeling off kilter. "Of course."

He wanted to date her, but he couldn't stay long enough to eat lunch? He made no sense.

When she returned with a white sack holding his food, he stood. His hand brushed hers as he took it, sending a sweet shiver through her.

"I packed a couple of cookies for you to sample, too," she said. "I once stayed in a hotel that offered fresh-baked cookies on arrival. Might be something to consider."

He dipped his head. "Thank you much. Like I said, nothing sexier than a smart woman."

With that, he turned and left her standing, watching the way he moved, confident and far too appealing.

April came up behind her. "Wow. He's quite the charmer. You sure you don't want to date him?"

Noelle glanced over her shoulder at her friend. "Just because he's a sweet-talker doesn't mean he won't break my heart."

She sighed. "No. But he might be worth a try."

Noelle turned to April, knowing that pain reflected in her gaze. She didn't want to be so afraid, but she couldn't help it. "How many times do I endure the heartache before I say it's enough?"

April wrapped an arm around her. "As many as it takes to find someone you love. There's nothing like having the person you love snuggle you at night or hold you when life gets tough."

But life was already tough. And she had no one. "I don't know. I just don't know."

Another customer arrived, interrupting their conversation. "Could you get this one? I need a moment."

"Sure, Noelle. No problem."

———

Noelle's nerves chattered on high-speed all afternoon. She burned two batches of chocolate chip cookies, forcing April to open the front and back doors to air out the shop so they wouldn't scare away their customers.

Right before six, she slipped into the bathroom. She tugged the band from her ponytail, letting her long hair slip around her shoulders in blond waves. The effect gave her a sexy, beachy look, and she quickly gathered it back into a ponytail. She added lip gloss, so that she didn't look so tired, and called it good.

She wasn't out to impress him. Just the opposite.

"Have fun," April called as she slipped out the door.

"Goodnight," Noelle said in response, grabbing the notes she'd compiled earlier in the day. Her meeting with Kade wasn't about fun. It was business.

She walked across the dirt parking lot, noticing the flat, brown dirt where the beautiful bluebells had once grown wild. She supposed at some point, she and the surrounding land would have to accept reality. The growth and prosperity of their town would come at a cost.

When she arrived, she was surprised to find a beautiful wooden door standing between her and the inside of the new motel. It looked like the construction company had taken the door from an old-fashioned rustic lodge. She pulled on the large iron handle, opening the way into Kade's world.

It was eerily quiet inside, and she assumed all the workers had gone home. The interior was in the finishing stages, with a fresh coat of paint on the walls, but the floor was still cement. The bottom portion of a luxurious front desk sat in place, but it lacked the countertop.

She stepped forward and ran her fingers along the detailed mahogany wood. Someone had serious craftsmanship skills. The beauty of the place seemed a little over the top for such a small town, but then again Kade came across as a man who took pride in what he did.

"Hello," she called out.

Sounds of movement came from down a hallway, and a few moments later, Kade appeared. "Hey. Come in and see the place."

He'd changed from the torn t-shirt he'd worn earlier into a

camel-colored Henley that enhanced his eyes and showcased his pecs. "What do you think?"

Noelle glanced around the room as though she hadn't spent the last few minutes surveying it. "It's beautiful, though I haven't quite forgiven you for mowing down the field of wildflowers."

"Oh," he frowned. "Definitely not a point in my favor."

"It's all right. There are still flowers out back." She couldn't stay mad at him now that she knew him. "I love the front desk."

He grinned. "Thanks. It's taken me some time to get it exactly how I wanted it. Wait until you see it with the forest green marble top I've ordered. It should be here by the weekend, and I'll install it then."

She widened her eyes in surprise. "Install it? You're building it yourself?"

He nodded, obviously proud of his work. "Woodworking is another hobby of mine."

She glanced from the counter to his eyes, bracing herself for the spark that would come when she made eye contact. And it did. "I'm impressed. How many hobbies do you have?"

A sexy half-smile tilted his lips. "That's one of my secrets."

Once again, he'd lulled her into a comfortable state. But it felt good, and she didn't want to fight it. "I can't convince you to give up any of your secrets?"

"Not yet. I barely know you," he teased.

She gave a soft laugh. She intended to keep her personal side protected as well. "Fair enough."

She held up the papers she'd printed out. "I brought a list of ideas and costs."

He took them from her. "Great. Let's sit back in the breakfast room. The tables were delivered yesterday."

Kade led the way around the corner and down a hallway

painted with a muted shade of sage green. The effect was inviting and soothing.

"I like the interior design," she said as she followed him. "It's more up-scale than I'd expected. What are you going to call this place?"

"I haven't decided yet, but I probably should, or I'll be opening without a sign."

He stopped at the entrance to a large room. "I wanted something comfortable and homey...and nice. A step up from a regular motel. Just because folks aren't in the big city doesn't mean they can't stay somewhere pleasant. I appreciate it when the places I stay are as beautiful as the surroundings. Most of my guests will be tourists who come for the fishing and families of Aspen's residents. I would like to help the town make a memorable impression."

She watched as he spoke, enjoying the way his face lit up as he talked. His enthusiasm spilled onto her. "I'm sure people will love it. But I'm curious how you find time to do everything."

He shrugged. "I make time for the things I enjoy. Life's too short to be unhappy." He sent her a pointed look.

"You're absolutely right. We should focus on what makes us happy." Like her friends and her shop.

He stepped aside to let her enter the room.

When she did, her gaze immediately snagged on the small table laden with sliced meats, cheeses, breads, and a bottle of wine. A vase full of pretty daisies sat off to the side.

The sight of the cozy, romantic setting put her on edge. "I thought we agreed we were only discussing business."

8

Kade shrugged and took Noelle's arm, trying to tug her inside. "You wouldn't let me take you to dinner, so I brought something here."

Noelle shook her head. "Kade, I don't—"

"It's food, Noelle. Nothing more. I get hungry this time of day and figured you did, too. I work better when my stomach isn't growling."

She still hesitated.

He sighed. "It's nothing more than an easy meal between friends. A chance to discuss business and maybe enjoy some conversation. I'm new in town and don't have many friends yet, which I'm trying to rectify. Can you consider it a friendly gesture? Like when April gave me chili today?"

She narrowed her gaze. "It seems more than that. You're a huge flirt."

He laughed then. "Hell, yes, I am. Can't help it. I like people. Like talking to them. Like helping them. What I'd really like to do right now is eat something and talk about how we can help each other." He gestured toward the table.

She *was* hungry, and she'd always found it difficult to turn down good cheese. He seemed honest in his declaration, and who couldn't use a new friend? "Okay. I'm sorry if I overreacted. I've already explained about my recent breakup."

"No explanations or apologies required." He held out a chair for her, and she sat. "Let's leave the past in the past."

She couldn't admit how much she longed to do exactly that. But she worried that if she forgot the past, she'd also forget the lessons she'd learned, and that would leave her open to more heartbreak.

Kade sat across from her and surveyed the silver tray of food between them. He lifted a piece of dark bread and laid slices of turkey and provolone on it. Afterward, he dipped his knife into what looked to be a cream cheese and cranberry mixture and spread it on top. Then he shoved the whole thing in his mouth.

"Mmm..." he said, nodding. "It's good."

Noelle followed his lead and made a bite-sized sandwich as well. She took a bite, and the ham and cheddar cheese melted on her tongue. "Where did you get this? Andersen's Grocery doesn't carry anything this fancy."

"I ordered it." He glanced at her with his engaging eyes. "I have a confession. I did have ulterior motives."

She stiffened, and he laughed. "Relax, sweetheart. I'm not hitting on you."

Noelle lifted her brow in question and watched as he poured them both a glass of wine and held one out to her. "Taste this."

She took it and sipped. The choice perfectly complemented their food. "It's very nice."

He sipped and agreed. "Great. Decision made then, and you didn't even know you were helping me."

A curious smile bubbled inside her. "What do you mean?"

"You obviously know food, right? And I needed help to decide what to serve at the open house. I had the caterer send over a selection of what I thought would work, and you confirmed my choices. You have good taste, by the way." He stuffed a slice of roast beef into his mouth.

"You are extremely sly, Kade Collier." And he made it so damn difficult to remain detached in his presence.

He grinned and nodded, encouraging her to do the same. "But in a good way, right?"

"I don't know about that." She lifted her glass and took another sip to hide her smile.

"It's all in good fun, and you seemed like you could use a little cheering up." He caught her gaze, his alive with energy. "Tell me you're not happier than you were a few days ago."

She snorted and shook her head, trying to keep the smile from her face. "Fine. I'm happier."

His expression took on a more serious note. "Good. My job is done."

She loved that he cared, but... "It's not your job to make me happy."

"Nope. It's not. Doesn't mean I can't try if I want to."

She studied him, the way his hair curled near his nape, the hint of a dimple in his right cheek when he smiled. "Thank you. It's good to know there are decent people in the world."

"Even if I'm a guy?" he teased.

She'd allow him that jab. He deserved it. "Even so."

He lifted his glass and swirled the liquid. "I've been where you are, Noelle. I know what it's like to hurt."

He'd said the words without meeting her gaze, but she didn't fail to notice the emotion behind them. She dropped her gaze and stared at her own glass, her emotions echoing his. "I guess none of us gets out unscathed."

"I guess not," he said with a sarcastic laugh and then straightened in his seat. "Which is why we need to eat good food, laugh with friends, and enjoy the hell out of life while we can."

She lifted her glass, embracing his point of view. "Here's to life, the good and the bad."

He gave her a brilliant smile and tapped his glass against hers. "Now you're talking."

9

Noelle handed Kade's morning coffee to him just like she had every morning since they'd come to an agreement on the services and products Rumors would provide the unnamed motel. "Here you go. The usual."

He lifted his brows in question. "Thanks. I guess I'll see you tonight?"

They were halfway through the series of classes, and she wouldn't miss it for the world. "Yep. I'll be there."

Whatever fear she'd had of him had disappeared. His unassuming, charming way made it impossible for her not to like him. She'd decided they were two people on similar paths in life, both with haunted pasts, both wanting a happy future. Nothing scary or dangerous there.

She couldn't deny her heart tugged on the strings of attraction every time he appeared, but it never needed to go beyond friendship. Honestly, she liked the idea of having a guy friend without worrying about the sticky mess of romance.

Kade gave her a warm smile and headed out the door.

April bumped her shoulder as she stepped next to her to

admire the view. "I don't know, Noelle. If I were you, I'd snag that one right up."

She frowned at her friend. "But you're not me. You don't have any idea what I've been through and how I feel."

April snorted. "Because having my cousin lie about sleeping with my boyfriend to break us up doesn't hurt. Nor does adopting her son to find out he's really Seth's son, and I'm the odd woman out."

Noelle sighed. Her friend and business partner had confided her secrets one day a few months back, and Noelle had been shocked. "But you and Seth found your way past that and have created a beautiful family."

April eyed her with a sassy look. "The point is, there were many times when I couldn't see that ever happening. There came a time when I had to have faith in the future and trust the man I loved. Life doesn't give us a crystal ball. Sometimes, we have to jump off the cliff without knowing where we'll land."

Noelle gave her friend a doubting look. "Aren't you the philosopher today?"

April laughed. "Hardly. But I see a good man coming in each day to see you, and you should give him a chance."

"He's not coming to see me." She shook her head as April's seed sprouted, making her wonder. "He's coming for coffee, like so many of our other customers."

"Our other customers don't look at you the way Kade does." She paused. "Except Gus. He does."

"Oh, Lord." Noelle snickered. Gus was forty years past his prime with white hairs that grew out of his ears and nose. "Not if he was the last man on earth."

"Then you'd better make a play for Kade, or that's what you'll be stuck with."

"I'd rather be alone." She'd considered it, planned what her future might be like if she found no one.

April scoffed. "Don't lie to me. I know you don't. So stop being so afraid to give it one more shot. Or more, if that's what it takes."

"I'll think about it." If she didn't give April at least that much, she'd never stop harassing her.

"You do that." April winked and headed for the backroom to start on the vegetable beef stew they'd serve that day.

Noelle might consider dating if Kade had continued to seem interested, but beyond the initial flirtations and the way she'd caught him watching her from time to time, he seemed as reserved as she was. They both needed a friend more than a lover right now. And, on second thought, she wasn't willing to risk what they had for something more that would likely end in disaster.

She made a mental note to return his shirt to him that evening, so his scent would no longer tempt her every night before she went to bed.

———

Kade pulled around to the back of the high school and was surprised to find his sister's car already parked near the bay doors. He pulled up next to her and exited his truck just as she did the same.

"Hey," he said as he walked forward to hug her.

She reciprocated. "You always give the best hugs."

"It's a specialty of mine."

He was the oldest in the family, and Krystal was stuck in the middle. He didn't know why, maybe because they both loved superhero movies, but he'd bonded more with her than with his other sisters. Krystal and he connected on a deeper level, and she seemed to understand him better than the rest of his family.

"You're here early," he said, looking at his watch, although he knew he had a good twenty minutes before class would start.

"I wanted to see you first. I need to leave early again tonight, so this is the only chance I'll have to talk to you."

He gestured for her to follow him to the side door. He unlocked it with a key the school had given him and let them both inside. "What's up?"

She shrugged, but pinned him with a look tinged with concern. "Hillary stopped at Mom's yesterday."

His muscles tensed involuntarily at the mention of his ex-wife's name. "What did she want?"

"She had some mail for you. She doesn't know your current address."

Why couldn't the woman just leave him alone? "Mom didn't give it to her, did she?"

Krystal rolled her eyes in exasperation. "No, but she told her you were in Aspen."

"Hell," he said under his breath. The last thing he needed was for Hillary to show up here and cause trouble.

Krystal pulled several envelopes from her purse. "Here."

Kade took them and scanned the return addresses. One appeared to be a solicitation. The other was a bill from the medical center in Pinecone. "It's been over a year. Why am I still getting this shit?"

Krystal gave him a consoling smile that did little to ease his pain. "I don't know. Hopefully, it will end soon. Do you need help to pay for anything?"

He shook his head as he gathered his resolve. "No. I have enough money."

Kade stuffed the envelopes in his back pocket and set about turning on the lights and getting his classroom ready to go.

Krystal helped him with the folding chairs. "You shouldn't

have to pay them all, anyway. Hillary should be equally responsible since you were married when..."

She didn't need to say it, and he especially didn't want to hear it. "I offered to cover all the payments. It was the cost of being free. Well-worth the money spent."

He would have given much more than that to have the opportunity to rebuild his life. Several thousand dollars didn't seem like much in comparison.

"I guess." Krystal put a hand on his shoulder and he met her gaze. "Things are better now, right?"

He gave her a reassuring smile. "Much better. You need to stop worrying about me. Life is good and getting better."

She lifted a cocky brow. "I sense a little something-something brewing between you and the blonde in our class. Noelle?"

He snorted and shook his head. "Just friends."

Krystal pushed her dark curls over her shoulder. "Are you sure? 'Cause I saw her checking out your butt last time in class. In fact, she had a hard time taking her eyes off you all night."

He grinned and nodded. "Can't say I mind hearing that."

His sister widened her eyes. "You should ask her out."

Kade covered his heart. "Did. She shot me down."

Laughter glittered in her eyes. "Ah. She friend-zoned you."

He didn't enjoy thinking she'd annihilated him before he'd decided if there could be something more. "What the hell does that mean?"

She drew a pretend circle over the ground. "As long as you stay in this area, meaning nothing sexual, she'll let you into her life. You step outside it?" She slid her finger across her neck.

He frowned. "Why does she get to decide? What if I don't agree?"

Krystal shrugged. "Then you take the chance of really pissing her off and losing her forever."

Why did women always seem to have control in relationships? "Great. A guy can't win these days."

She laughed. "Could you ever?"

He shook his head and turned at the sound of a car approaching.

———

Noelle pulled in front of the high school's bay door and left her car running. She'd barely stepped from the driver's seat when Kade walked from the open bay.

"Should I pull my car inside again?" she asked.

He gave her a smile that sent warm shivers racing through her. "Definitely."

He directed her inside and was there to open her door when she shoved the gearshift into park. He pulled on the door handle, and she grimaced at the sound of metal grating on metal.

"It just started doing that," she said as she climbed out.

"You need to grease it."

Like that made any sense to her. "Okay."

He captured her gaze and held it. Then another smile tilted his lips. "Do you know how?"

"No." She sighed. "Is there anyone who knows less about cars than me?"

He unfolded his fingers as he counted. "My mom. Most of my sisters. Plenty of guys out there are clueless, too, but maybe not as clueless as you."

"Thanks," she said with a heavy dose of sarcasm.

"The shop has most of the lubricants you'll need. If you want to hang around after class, I'll take care of you."

She stared at him, trying to read his expression, wondering if he'd meant that as a flirty double entendre. But he kept his features straight for several seconds and then smiled, still not giving her a certain answer.

"Sure," she said, suddenly wanting to tease him back. "It's been a while, and you've been dying to get your hands on my chassis, so I might as well let you."

He groaned with mock anguish and flattened a hand on his chest. "You're killing me, girl."

Heated attraction flared inside her, and she hid it with a laugh. "You're not the only one who can compare cars to sex."

His gaze held, twisting her insides into something deliciously uncomfortable. "Mmm... My two favorite things."

She blinked and looked away. This was a game she wouldn't win. She might toss a few innuendoes his way, but he was the master of flirtation, and her heart would cave before he gave in. "I'm going to say hello to your sister."

"You do that," he said as she walked away. She could feel his gaze burning her with each step she took.

"Week four," she said as she approached Krystal, who occupied one of the folding chairs.

Krystal stowed her phone in her pocket and smiled. "More adventures for us."

Now that Noelle knew Kade was her brother, it surprised her she hadn't noticed the similarities between them before. The deep brown eyes, the slight dimple when she smiled. The naturally upbeat attitude. "I can't wait. Honestly, I should have taken this type of class years ago."

Krystal's eyes brightened. "Ha, me, too. I've always relied on my brother or dad to take care of everything. But I had to spend the night on the side of the road between here and Salt Lake a few months back when my tire went flat and there was no cell service. I was so afraid of asking anyone to help me I hid in my car until morning. You never know which strangers you can trust."

Noelle blew out a breath as an unwanted memory surfaced. "I know that better than I'd like. After I turned eighteen, I wanted to move back to Aspen, so I hitched a ride with a trucker. I know, dumb. We were almost here when he decided I owed him payment for the ride. He pulled over and thought I'd willingly get into the back of his cab with him." She frowned, remembering how frightened she'd been.

Krystal narrowed her eyes in concern. "Oh, Noelle. He could have *raped* you."

She gave a sarcastic laugh. "I'm pretty sure that was his intention. And I have no idea why I told you that." She shook her head, wishing she could erase her last few sentences. She'd been so naïve when she'd been younger. Some things she'd done had been downright idiotic.

Krystal gave her a gentle smile. "I have that effect on people."

"Yes, she does," Kade said, startling Noelle. She hadn't heard him walk up behind them. "Be careful, or she'll blackmail you with what you tell her."

Krystal waved him away. "That's only for you, dear brother. Your secret is safe with me, Noelle."

"Secret?" he said, lifting a brow.

Noelle gave him a furtive glance. "It looks like you're not the only one."

He narrowed his brown eyes and nodded slowly. "Hmm... How about I'll tell you my secrets if you'll tell me yours?"

"Don't fall for it, Noelle," Krystal said. "Or if you do, make sure he goes first. He's been known to cheat on that one."

He snorted. "I was twelve, Krystal. Twelve."

"And I still haven't forgiven you," she teased.

Warmth bubbled inside Noelle as she watched the two siblings interact. It was obvious they cared about each other, and she had no doubt they were both decent people. People she could care about.

The sound of female voices drew their attention toward the open bay doors as Nancy and Betty walked in.

"Looks like the rest of the class is here," Kade said as he headed to greet his students.

———

By the end of class, Noelle and the other ladies had learned to replace windshield wipers, along with how to check their oil, check their antifreeze, and add washer fluid. Betty and Nancy gushed to Kade about how helpful the class was before they headed out, and Noelle agreed. Krystal had left with apologies fifteen minutes earlier, and suddenly Noelle wished she hadn't agreed to stay after.

"You don't have to help me with my car," she said as her nerves coiled tighter. "I'm sure if I drop it off at Walt's in the morning, he'd be happy to do it for me."

Kade closed the distance between them and tugged at her black t-shirt near her belly button in a playful gesture. "Yes, but then you wouldn't know how to do it next time, and I wouldn't get the chance to mess with your car."

Her breath caught as she inhaled. She'd tried to keep him framed as a friend all evening, but she'd had a hard time ignoring the tight fit of his ripped jeans. Or how his muscles had flexed as he'd helped the ladies lift the hoods of their cars.

He took her hand and tugged her toward her Mustang. "Come on. It won't take long."

10

The feel of Kade's roughened fingers wrapped around her hand sent desire streaking through Noelle like cracks on a broken windshield. She wanted to pull from him, but couldn't. He felt too good, too right.

He stopped at the hood of her Mustang and caught her gaze as he released her hand. "What?" he asked, as though she'd spoken to him.

She smiled, though her heart raced a million miles an hour. "I didn't say anything."

"No, but you're thinking something."

She shook her head. "I was just thinking about my car."

"Yeah," he said thoughtfully. "Me, too."

He glanced across the garage and then back to her. "Hang tight a minute. Let me gather some supplies."

He moved away from her, and she immediately felt the loss. "Oh, God," she whispered under her breath. She was headed down the same painful path she'd taken far too many times, and she didn't know how to stop. Didn't think she wanted to know, either.

She wanted to like Kade.

But she didn't want to like him.

Who was she kidding? She already liked him. How could she not? His beautiful eyes had distracted her while his smile and laugh had snuck in the back way and stolen her heart. She was her own worst enemy.

Now, what did she do? She couldn't walk away, not until he'd proven he wasn't worthy. She knew that much.

The fact was, she was stuck. Until he broke her heart or until she pushed him away. As much as she wanted to deny it, and she had, she *wanted* to be in love, wanted a man to hold her tight while they kissed, while they laughed, or if she cried.

With him looking at her the way he did and treating her like she was special, she couldn't ignore the opportunity that he *might* be the one.

As he walked toward her carrying several cans, her insides tightened with attraction, with desire.

"I've got you covered. One for your door." He held up a blue can before setting it on the nearby workbench. "One for your locks, and another for your latches." His flirtatious smile was back, and she was helpless against it. "But first, I want you to let me look under your hood."

She knew teasing him in return would send the message that she was open to him. The thought thrilled and frightened her. "Maybe," she said with a laugh.

A sexy, confident smile tugged at his lips. "I think you'll let me."

He was right. She narrowed her eyes playfully and headed for the front of the car. She reached for the lever by the grille and released it. It opened with a pop, and she was grateful that at least she knew where that was.

"Wow," he said, gazing at her engine. "This is a mess." He drew a finger along something metal before holding up the greasy stain to her.

She shrugged. "Cars are supposed to be dirty. It's not like you're going to eat off it."

Not once in her life had she heard of someone cleaning an engine. Though, she had to admit, none of her friends were mechanics or married to one.

He walked toward her with his finger still in the air. "Oh, sweetheart. This car is a classic, don't you know? It's not the family sedan. If you want her to purr, you need to treat her right." He stopped when he was only inches from her and aimed his finger toward her nose.

She grabbed his hand to stop him from touching her as another shot of excitement drilled through her. "Don't," she said with a laugh.

He twisted their hands until he held hers. He gripped it with his other hand and then drew his greasy finger down the underside of her forearm until he stopped on her pulse that raced beneath his finger. A black streak marked his path. "You're not afraid to get dirty, are you?"

She inhaled, sending her breasts rising toward him as she tried to contain her thundering heartbeat. "I don't even know how to answer that. I think you're talking about something other than cars."

He studied her for a long moment, his gaze growing serious. "Maybe I am."

She swallowed, and emotion clogged her throat. "I don't want to be hurt again," she whispered. She wished she could be fearless, like she'd been at one time, but life had changed her.

"I know," he whispered. "Me, either. But I can't stop thinking about you, can't stop thinking about how it would feel to kiss you."

Her lungs faltered.

He held her gaze as he wiped his finger on a shop rag he had tucked in his pocket. "I'm going to kiss you, Noelle, unless you ask me to stop."

Even if she could breathe well enough to speak, she wouldn't have stopped him. She ached for the feel of his lips on hers, ached for him to wrap her in his strong embrace.

When she didn't answer, he moved closer, pulling her against him. She swallowed as the glorious feeling of being held overwhelmed her. He lifted his hands, slid his thumbs in front of her ears, and tenderly cradled her face. He studied her eyes and then tilted his head.

She trembled as his lips crossed hers. Soft at first. Then more demanding. She wrapped her arms around his back, feeling his warmth, breathing in his unforgettable scent.

He ran his tongue along her bottom lip, and she opened her mouth, allowing him inside. The act was like gasoline on a lingering fire, and need exploded inside her. She gripped his shirt as he commanded their kiss, leaving her soft and aching for him.

A minute later, he broke the kiss and crushed her to his chest. "Damn."

"What?" she asked, breathless.

A guilty grin spilled across his lips. "I was kind of hoping there would be nothing there."

His answer surprised her, and she pushed away from him. "You didn't want to enjoy kissing me?" She wasn't sure how she felt about that. "Then why did you?"

"I needed to know. If there was nothing there, then I could stop thinking about you."

"But?" Her heart thudded in anticipation of his answer.

"But, this." He pulled her hard against him and claimed her mouth with a fierce kiss. She slid her hands over his wide shoulders and into his hair, returning what he offered her.

When her lungs screamed for air, she put a hand to his

cheek, her fingers grazing the short stubble, and she ended the kiss, leaning away to see him better. He held her with his gaze, and she looked deep into his eyes. Her thoughts tumbled over each other as she searched for the truth that only his expression could tell her.

He wanted her.

God, she wanted him, too.

"I don't know what I'm going to do with you," he whispered, tracing a thumb down her cheek, seeming as nervous as she did.

"Because?"

He slowly shook his head. "Because I wasn't looking for this either."

She lifted her brows. "Should I ask why?" What if he *was* married? She hadn't considered that he might be. Or maybe he had a serious girlfriend. Her stomach muscles tightened, preparing for an emotional blow. "You're not taken, are you?"

"No."

Her tension eased a little. "Not married?" she asked, just to be sure.

"Divorced."

She nodded as the breath she'd been holding eased out of her. "I'm sorry."

He tucked a strand of hair behind her ear. "Me, too." Then he met her gaze and smiled. "But life goes on."

"Can I ask what happened?"

A flash of pain darkened his eyes. "We lost a baby, and our marriage couldn't withstand the devastation."

"You had a child?" The thought of him with another woman, with a baby... "I'm so sorry."

He studied her face as he ran his forefinger across her bottom lip. Then he leaned toward her.

His kiss was warm and tender, reigniting the sparks inside.

"If we don't get started on your car, we won't finish. Are you okay if I turn on the music? I work better with tunes."

"Sure," she said as he pulled away. He'd shared a part of himself with her, but obviously not all.

He sauntered across the bay to an old stereo system and turned it on. She recognized the haunting song that filled the air. The singer crooned about getting lost in a woman and whiskey, and the music had a gritty, edgy beat that suited her mood perfectly.

It seemed they both had pasts hanging over them as they struggled to move forward. Knowing that about him eased her fears. He understood.

She followed to where he ended up, at her driver's side door with the blue can in his hand.

"Watch and learn, sweetheart." He pulled the lid from the can and sprayed it on the hinge. Then he swung her door back and forth a few times, and the squeaking stopped. "Not hard at all."

She stuck her finger in a hole near the bottom of his shirt and tugged. He met her gaze, his own dark and unreadable. "Thank you for helping me with this. I really appreciate it."

His expression warmed. "No problem. I like helping people." He paused. "I really like helping you."

She couldn't stop her grin. Somehow, he'd climbed her walls and snuck in past the radar. But now that he was there, she couldn't regret it. "Are you going to show me how to lube the rest?"

"Absolutely. Anytime you're ready."

11

By the time Kade had finished, he'd helped her remove all the noisy squeaks from her car. At the moment, he had her applying a graphite lubricant to her door locks. He allowed his gaze to linger on her as she leaned over to slide the key in the keyhole.

"That's it," he said as he traced her curves. She'd been more than he'd expected, more than he'd wanted, but damn if she wasn't there. In his life, in his work, creeping her way into his heart.

It scared the hell out of him to think of getting close to another person. The two that he'd loved beyond measure were gone. One was a ghost, the other a shell where his wife used to be. But she'd made that choice, preferring the comfort of drugs, alcohol, and another man to his arms.

A guy could only fight so hard for so long.

Maybe God had decided he'd suffered enough. Maybe he could go on to love again.

Noelle turned to him with a smile. "I got it."

"You did. But look at you, you're a mess."

She grinned and held up her greasy hands. The sight of her

loose blond curls hanging over one shoulder as excitement glowed in her eyes buried her barbs deep in his heart. "And you thought I was afraid to get dirty."

He couldn't resist pulling her to him. "I should have known."

She laughed and held her hands outward. "I'm going to get grease all over you."

He leaned in and tasted her lips one more time. "Do you think I care?"

She held out for a few moments, allowing him to kiss her as he ran his hands over her hips and cupped her ass, taking advantage of the situation. He savored the feeling of having a woman in his arms once again.

Noelle caved and hugged his neck, spurring his desire even more.

A slow song from his high school days came on the radio, reminding him of a carefree time before the harsh realities of life had crept in. He broke their kiss and began to move them to the slow beat.

She gave a soft laugh, but didn't resist.

"I used to love this song," he whispered. Her hair was soft against his lips and smelled sweet and sexy at the same time.

"Me, too. It's been forever since I've heard it."

"Yeah." He dipped her over his arm.

She laughed and grabbed for his shirt. "You'll drop me."

"Never." Even now, he wondered how he'd let her go.

She shook her head as though she disagreed, but smiled, and he brought her upright. He held her soft body against his, wondering if it was his imagination or his need to be with a woman that made her seem so perfect. Or maybe he'd lucked out this time.

"It's almost midnight," she said, her voice quiet.

He glanced at the clock near the bay doors. "I can't believe it's so late. What time did everyone else leave?"

"Eight." She seemed as surprised as he did that the time had flown as fast as it had. They'd been alone together for four hours, and it seemed like minutes.

"I have to be at work at six in the morning," she added.

He sighed. "I have to be in early, too. The county building inspector is coming by for a preliminary inspection."

She ran her hands over his shoulders and down his biceps, her gaze following her fingers. Then she looked back at him. "Will you have time for coffee?"

He could sense the uncertainty in her voice and hated whoever had placed that doubt there. "I'll always have time for coffee. And for you."

She raised her brows, happiness chasing away the skepticism in her pretty blue eyes. That was how it should be. "Okay. I should go."

"I'm going to follow you again." She couldn't stop him.

She searched his gaze. "I know," she whispered.

He took her face between his hands again, holding her gaze as he lowered his lips to hers. Her eyelids fluttered shut, driving cupid's arrow deep within his heart.

———

The next morning, Kade parked near the front of his motel and jumped out of his truck. A middle-aged man wearing denim and carrying a clipboard waited by the front door, looking none too happy. Kade had meant to be at the worksite first thing that morning, but the sewer system had backed up at his parents' house, and his dad was out of town. Family duty called.

He hurried toward the man with wiry, gray hair hanging

below the inspector's official cap. "Sorry, I'm running behind. There are workers inside. You could have gone in and started."

He met his gaze without smiling. "I never do an inspection without the owner present."

Kade wanted to tell him to lighten up, but that wouldn't help matters. "I had family problems."

"Don't we all?" He squinted at his clipboard, deepening the crow's feet around his eyes. "Let's get on with this. I'm already behind schedule."

Kade hoped his tardiness wouldn't make the guy more critical during the inspection. He wanted his building safe, but didn't want to have to plow through layers of red tape to get it there. "Sure thing."

He opened the door for the inspector as he glanced toward Rumors. Noelle would wonder about him, he knew. He'd wanted to call from his parents' house, but didn't have her number. He hadn't expected to ask for it, ever. But then the unexpected happened.

Just as he had that thought, he realized he could have found the number for Rumors and called her at the shop. He mentally kicked himself as he followed the inspector inside.

Later, when he explained, he'd find out how reasonable and forgiving Noelle could be. It killed him to know he'd bring doubt back to her heart, but all he could do now was wait out the inspector and then beg for her forgiveness.

"Uh-oh." The older man said forty minutes later and stopped quickly, staring at his clipboard.

Kade almost plowed into the back of him, where he stood near the front desk. They'd made it through most of the building with only a few minor issues.

Unease trickled through Kade. The man seemed much too happy when he'd spoken. "Is there a problem?"

"Your permit is only for twenty units." He looked at him from beneath lowered brows. "You've built thirty."

Kade frowned. "We fixed that. I took the paperwork to the courthouse myself. Paid the additional fee."

The inspector flipped through a couple of papers. "Well, it's not showing here."

Son of a bitch.

The man stared at him with a dull expression. "Did you hold a public hearing?"

Kade folded his arms. "No. They didn't inform me that I needed to."

"Hmm...well." He turned the clipboard around and held out a pen to Kade. "Sign here that you've been notified of everything I've found. You'll need to make repairs or additions to bring it into compliance. And you're going to need to follow up on that change to the building license before you'll be able to open. I wouldn't sit on it either. That red tape can get kind of sticky and hard to move sometimes."

He grabbed the pen and scrawled over the bottom of the page. The inspector pulled off the pink copy and handed it to him. "Have a nice day."

Kade stared after him as he walked out the door. *"Damn it to hell,"* he muttered.

12

A weighted cloud hung over Noelle, turning the sunny, early October day dismal. Outside of her shop, everything looked bright, but inside her heart, the shadows of her past chased her.

She'd been so hyped after her evening with Kade that she hadn't been able to sleep. She'd wrapped herself in his shirt and climbed under the covers, but she couldn't get the taste of him out of her mind.

She wanted more.

The only way she'd managed to get any sleep was the knowledge that she'd see him this morning. Only she hadn't. It was three hours past his usual appearance, and each minute had been agony.

"Got those?" April asked.

Noelle glanced down and realized she'd soaked the cinnamon rolls with icing. She dropped the tube of icing and lifted the sheet to put them in the display case. "I'm done."

April tilted her head, peering at Noelle's face. "Something's wrong."

"Nah." She shook her head. "I'm good."

In her excitement that morning, she'd spilled the details of the previous evening to her friend. April had been thrilled, and so had Noelle. At the time, anyway.

April put a hand on her arm. "Don't judge him yet."

Noelle snorted as tears gathered behind her eyelids. She blinked rapidly, forcing them away.

Her friend patted her. "You don't know what might have happened. Give it a little time. I know he likes you, and I know it's hard, but be patient."

Noelle sighed as she turned toward the kitchen. The door chimed as she stepped through the doorway, but she wouldn't bother to look. If she'd have been smart, she would have ignored her heart and listened to her brain.

She opened the fridge to place the remaining icing inside. When she closed the door, strong arms wrapped around her waist from behind, startling her.

"I'm sorry," Kade whispered into her ear.

She turned and searched his face, looking for a sign that he was about to tell her goodbye. She couldn't see it, but she didn't trust her judgment any longer.

He shook his head as distress reflected in his eyes. "I've had an awful morning."

She couldn't shut down her heart, no matter how much she wanted to. "What happened?"

"The worst thing? I couldn't get over here to kiss you good morning, but I'm going to fix that now." He didn't wait for a response before he lowered his head to hers and claimed a kiss that first soothed and then excited her.

He stopped. Then kissed her again. "There. That's better."

She smiled up at him, and the tension in his body seemed to leave.

"I'm so sorry I couldn't come earlier. My parents' sewer backed up into their house, and my dad's not home. I spent the morning helping my mom deal with that mess. I wanted to call, but didn't have your number."

He pulled his cell phone from his pocket and handed it to her. "That's the next problem on my list to fix."

"Okay." She focused on his phone and put her number in his contact list. His excuse made perfect sense, and she'd been worried for nothing. She exhaled a weighted breath and handed the phone back to him. "Is your mom okay?"

"Yeah, I did damage control and helped her call her insurance man. She's always relied heavily on my dad for stuff like this, so she's kind of helpless when he's not around."

She snorted. "Like me."

He ran his hands down her arms, leaving goose bumps in his wake. "Nothing like you. You might not know everything, but you're strong, and you're not afraid."

Many things frightened her. Many challenges she was certain she'd never overcome. "I don't know about that."

"I wish you could see what I see. You're strong and beautiful and smart." He leaned in and kissed the spot in front of her ear. "And sexy."

If she'd had any remaining reserves, his words melted them away. "And you're a charmer."

He nodded and grinned. "That is possible."

"More than possible. You with your delicious brown eyes and honeyed words. It's a wonder I held out as long as I did."

"I was surprised, too," he teased. "I'm kind of hard to resist."

She slipped a hand behind his head and pulled him toward her. "Yes, you are." She kissed him, molding her body against his, enjoying his heated response.

"Damn," he whispered. "What I wouldn't give to steal you away from here and pretend I didn't have a mountain of problems waiting for me."

She tilted her head in question. "Something else besides your mom?"

"Apparently so. My original plans for the motel included only twenty units. But when I sat down with my contractor, the cost ended up being less than I expected, and he convinced me to go bigger. He was right. Pinecone has seen some significant growth, and it's spilling into Aspen."

"It is. I hate to see it happen too fast, but people are discovering the little town and all it offers."

He held her gaze. "People like me."

She winced. "I didn't mean to make it sound like I didn't want you here. Just not everyone else." She gave him a repentant smile and hoped he understood what she meant.

He sighed. "Long story short, I applied for a change in the building permit, but it somehow didn't get completed. I'm not sure who dropped the ball. That's what I'll be figuring out today. I need to head to the county offices in Pinecone and do a little digging. The inspector said my change would require a minimum of a public hearing to see if there are any objections." He glanced at her. "From people like you."

She laughed. "You did plow right over the beautiful field of wildflowers that used to grow next door."

He pointed to himself. "But look what you got instead."

"True." Looking at it from that perspective, she would have gladly given them up. His lot wasn't the only place in town where they grew. If she needed to see bluebells, she could take a walk down Main Street or drive to the outskirts of town.

Kade gave her another quick kiss before he released her. "Anyway, I have to go. I don't know how long it's going to take me to wade through it all, if I can even make any headway today."

She didn't want him to leave. "Okay."

He lifted hopeful brows that ignited her heart. "Can I see you later?"

"Yeah. Call me when you're free. I'll be in the shop until four."

"You got it." He kissed her again. "I'm going to want more of this later on."

"Me, too."

He hugged her tightly before he left, and she missed him the instant he was gone.

She turned and surveyed the kitchen, trying to remember what was next on her list. Before she could get to it, her phone rang.

She pulled her phone from her apron and glanced at the unfamiliar number. "Hello?"

Kade's chuckle came over the line. "I wanted to make sure you had my number, too. I won't chance another miscommunication."

Her heart overflowed. "Thank you. I'll save it to my contacts now."

"Okay." He paused, as though he needed a moment to consider his words. "Have a good day, sweetheart."

"You, too. I hope everything works out."

"It will. As long as I can see you tonight."

———

The minutes ticked by for Noelle, each second making certain she noticed it before moving on to the next. When four o'clock finally rolled around, she threw her apron into the laundry basket and said her goodbyes, eager to get on with her evening.

Luckily, April would stay until six before she closed the shop. At some point, they'd probably want to consider hiring someone to work later into the evening. But for now, the citizens of Aspen seemed happy with their current operating hours. She and April made a decent profit, and they both enjoyed their downtime.

By the time she reached home, she hadn't heard from Kade. So she jumped into the shower, wanting to rinse off the day's work and be fresh for her date later.

She picked up her phone after she'd blow-dried her hair, afraid she might not have heard his call over the noise.

No calls, but a text popped up. *Have you eaten dinner?*

The question brought a smile to her face. She glanced at the clock, finding it was nearly six. *No.*

Wait for me. I'll be there in forty-five.

Want me to cook? she responded.

No.

She bit her bottom lip, enjoying their exchange. *Do you need my address?*

I know where you live, sweetheart.

Okay. She added a smiley face.

He didn't reply, and she still had close to an hour to wait, during which she might go stir-crazy. She settled on painting her toenails to keep the insanity at bay.

She couldn't get over the thought that everything in her life had changed. At least it felt that way. Could love really be this easy? She drew the brush covered with bright pink polish over her pinky toenail.

It had never been for her in the past. But then, maybe she hadn't really been in love with Tyler or Ian.

It was too soon to tell with Kade. But whatever was growing between them seemed much stronger than what she'd had with either of her past two boyfriends. Her feelings for him were... deeper, richer, and they seemed to connect on an indefinable level.

He respected her, and he made sure she knew she mattered.

Her laugh came so easily with him, and she couldn't think of anything she'd rather do than be with him. It wouldn't matter where she was as long as he was with her.

A look, his touch, a kiss excited her beyond belief, and she wanted nothing more than to make him smile and laugh, too.

Was that love?

13

Thirty-five minutes later, a vehicle pulled into Noelle's drive, and she peeked out her lace curtains to see Kade emerging from his silver Ford. Tingling excitement rushed through her.

Ever since their first kiss, she'd longed to be alone with him again.

She opened the front door to her little house just as he reached the bottom of the porch. He didn't slow his stride. He took both steps in one swoop and pulled her into his arms. Before she had a chance to say hello, he had his mouth on hers, hungry and demanding.

She swooned inside, allowing him to carry her away with his passion.

"Wow," she said, breathless after their kiss.

He grinned as he watched her with his heart-melting eyes. "I missed you."

"I'd say so." She laughed. "I missed you, too."

"Good." He glanced beyond her into the house. "Do you need to do anything before we leave, or are you ready?"

"I'm ready." More than. "What are we doing?"

"How do you feel about the stars?"

She glanced toward the heavens. The night sky was at least an hour away, and a slight chill hung in the air, crisp and invigorating. Good thing she'd worn a jacket. The day had been warm, but the October evenings brought cooler temperatures with them. "I love the stars."

"There's a meteor shower tonight. One of the closest this year. With no moon, we ought to see it very well. I grabbed some chicken and potato salad to eat while we watch. Are you okay with that?"

She lifted her shoulders and smiled. "Sounds like fun."

No one had ever taken the time to show her the stars. It seemed like a lovely, romantic idea, and she enjoyed being romanced. "Should I bring blankets?"

"I've got it covered."

He waited for her to pull the door shut behind her, and then took her hand and led her down the steps. When they reached his truck, he opened the passenger door and helped her inside before running around to the driver's side. The interior was nice. Leather. The smell of the seats, mixed with the scent of his cologne, created a heady concoction.

"I thought you liked classic cars," she said as he started the engine.

"I do."

"Then why the new truck? You should drive one of those fancy old ones."

A spark of mischief lit in his eyes. "As a matter of fact, I own a 1956 Ford F100 that's pretty sweet. But it's not so nice to drive back and forth between here and Pinecone. If I'm trying to impress a lady—which I am, in case you couldn't tell—this truck is much more comfortable. But I'll take you for a ride in

Betty Lou one of these days, too. I also have a '68 Camaro, and I wouldn't mind adding a Mustang to my collection." He lifted his brows in a teasing manner.

"I'm not selling her. I love my convertible." Much more now that he was interested in her car, too.

"I guess as long as you'll let me tinker around with her, I'll have to be satisfied with that."

He patted the seat next to him, and she slid over. He slipped his hand between her knees and held onto her there as he drove toward the road that would take them higher into the hills.

When they were far enough away from the small town's lights, he pulled to the side of the road in a grassy area and killed the engine. The sun glowed orange as it hovered near the horizon, and there wasn't another soul around as far as she could see.

"Come on," Kade said, tugging her out his door.

She slid over, and he held out his arms, helping her down from his truck. Kade held her hand as he walked to the tailgate and then climbed on the bumper before lowering his hand to her. She was glad she'd worn jeans instead of a skirt, too.

She put a foot on the bumper and let him haul her upwards. They both stepped over the tailgate into the back of the truck.

Just behind the cab, he'd tied down two sleeping bags and a plastic sack. He opened the sleeping bags, and she helped him spread them in the back of the truck, creating a soft bed. Then they both sat down together, and he emptied the sack.

The scent of fried chicken wafted toward her as he set a plastic bag filled with a roasted chicken between them. He had another sack containing two rolls, along with a disposable container of potato salad.

"Did you get this from the deli at Andersen's?"

"Yep. It might not look like much, but it's good."

"It looks great." She smiled at what he considered a meal. He was such a man. Not a fruit or vegetable among the items unless she counted the potatoes, but she found the spread delightful.

He handed a wrapped package of plastic ware to her. "Sorry, I didn't think to grab plates."

She shrugged. "We don't need them. I've eaten plenty of meals with just my fingers." She opened the top of the chicken bag and pulled off a piece of meat with her fork.

He slid a sideways glance toward her. "How many is plenty?"

She met his look with a confused one of her own.

He lifted his chin, encouraging her. "You said you'd eaten plenty of meals with your fingers. Why not use a fork?"

She tilted her head as she thought about how to explain things. She didn't want the pity she knew would follow, but her past was her past. "When I was little, before my mom left, I often made my own meals, and it was just as easy to use my fingers to eat. Then there was a period after I turned eighteen and I was on my own that I didn't own a plate or a fork." She gave a sad laugh, so grateful that part of her life was in the past.

He tilted his head in question as though he doubted her sincerity. "Seriously?"

She focused on her chicken. "It happens. Not all of us are blessed with good moms."

Kade exhaled a deep sigh. "Damn, Noelle. That's rough."

She smiled because she could now. "It *was* rough. But that part of my life is over. If you count the utensils at Rumors, I have more than enough forks to last me a lifetime."

He took her hand and squeezed. "Like I said, you're a smart woman. How old were you when your mom took off?"

She stuck her fork into the potato salad and scooped some. "Four."

"*Four?* You made your own meals at four?"

She shrugged. "Three, four. A hungry kid can be pretty resourceful." Most people couldn't remember things from that young of an age, but she had clear memories of eating boxed cereal while sitting on the kitchen floor. "Though I have no idea who fixed my bottles when I was a baby."

The look on his face churned her pain. "Have you ever tried to find her, now that you're an adult?"

She met his gaze square on. "Why would I want to? She's nothing to me."

He blinked. "Right. Someone who would do something like that to a child... I wouldn't give a person like that the time of day, either."

If he didn't stop, he'd make her cry. "She doesn't deserve any more of our date time, either." She lifted another forkful of potato salad and held it out to him.

He grinned and ate it, and she felt like she could breathe again. "What did you find out today about your building permit?"

"They fucked it up," he said in a vehement tone, and then quickly met her gaze. "Excuse the language."

She shrugged. "Don't worry about it. I've tossed a few cuss words to the wind from time to time."

He nodded in appreciation as he pulled out a bottle of water and a bottle of beer and offered both to her. She took the beer. He did the same.

Kade twisted off the cap with a hiss. "It was as I thought. I'd completed my portion, but they'd dropped the ball. They'll put out public hearing notices within the next two weeks. The office staff promised me they'd speed up the process as much as possible so that it won't affect my opening. I'm a little worried, though."

"Why's that?"

He sucked in a breath and tilted his head. "I had the pleasure of having one of the council members drop by while I was in their office. An old dude who's been serving way too long. He overheard the conversation and butted in. He had the nerve to chastise me, saying I was trying to work the system, trying to shove a bigger motel down Aspen's throats when they'd originally agreed to license a smaller one. I think he's losing his mind."

She suspected she knew the culprit. "Dave Jackson?"

"That's the guy."

The rumor mills had gone wild a few months back, saying he'd propositioned the local librarian in Pinecone. His office had passed it off as a joke, but many still doubted his mental stability. "Many people have recently questioned his ability to lead. Unfortunately, he has money, and no one wants to challenge him. He's just crazy enough to be dangerous."

Kade finished his drink of beer. "Exactly. I'm hoping I'm too small to hold his interest for long."

She sent him a commiserating look. "I'm sorry. Owning a business has its benefits, but it can be a pain, too."

His frustration turned into a smile. "Absolutely."

Only a few wisps of light danced in the sky by the time they'd finished eating. They packed up the remains of their dinner, and he leaned against the bed of the truck. He held open his arms. "Come here."

She settled against him, feeling safe and sound.

He kissed her hair. "There's a performance at the outdoor theater in Pinecone next week. Would you like to go? It's the last one of the season."

She'd only gone once years ago with Kimber, but she'd enjoyed it immensely. "I'd love to."

"Good. Second question. What do you think about coming

to my house sometime this week and letting me work on your engine? I've been itching to clean it up."

She laughed. "You can't stand it, can you?"

He chuckled. "No. I admit I love a new project."

She leaned on his shoulder and looked up at him. "Only if you'll let me bring dinner. I could make us some soup and breadsticks at work."

Kade put his fingers under her chin and tilted her head until she was close enough to kiss. "I love your soup."

I love you hovered on the tip of her tongue, but she couldn't say it. It was too soon to voice it. Too soon to think about it.

He kissed her then, stirring the warm glow inside her that had been present all evening. She shifted in his arms until he held most of her weight and she had one knee over his thighs. She was still in an awkward position, but this way, she could hold on to him.

His kiss was long and slow, and she savored the taste. She drew her fingers along his neck and into his soft hair. Energy hummed between them, strong and sweet, increasing with each second.

She ended their kiss when her position grew uncomfortable, and she shifted even more.

He waited until she'd situated herself before he wrapped his arm around her. "Sorry. A truck bed isn't the best place to kiss a girl."

That he was concerned for her comfort touched her heart.

Still, she knew as well as most, if a guy took a girl to a remote location, he had ulterior motives. At the very least, he'd kiss her well and good.

He might even try for more.

It might surprise Kade to know that was okay with her. More than okay. She'd craved his touch, had for a while now, and though she couldn't give her heart away yet, she wanted to know what it was like to have him hold her. Another layer of compatibility that needed to fit.

She turned and crawled onto his lap, straddling him, enjoying the surprised look in his eyes. "A truck bed works just fine if you do it right."

14

Noelle grinned at the surprised look on Kade's face as she sat on his lap, wrapped her arms around his neck, leaving their faces mere inches apart. "How's this? Can you kiss me properly now?"

"Hell, yes." He took her jaw, tilting her head as he brushed his lips against hers. Softly. Then more demanding.

He grew hard against her, and she scooted closer so that he fit her snuggly. They had too many clothes between them, but she wanted to savor the anticipation of what was to come. Too often, she'd encouraged Ian to hurry to the next step, wanting to get to the heart of lovemaking.

Not this time. She wanted each moment to be excruciatingly delicious. The feel of his soft lips. The slide of his tongue against hers. The way each kiss sent a shock to her core, leaving her heated and aching.

When he ended their kiss, she gasped as a tremble rolled through her.

"You know I want you," Kade said, his voice husky, his eyes hot with desire.

"I know," she whispered, running a thumb over his bottom lip. "I want you, too."

"Are we rushing things?"

She loved that he worried about it. "I don't think so. It feels right." So very right.

"It does."

She touched his bottom lip with the tip of her finger. "What if we pretend we've never had broken hearts? What if this is what it is, and it's good? Better than good?"

"Noelle." He whispered her name as he studied her eyes, his full of tender emotion and desire.

He held out for a moment before he unzipped her jacket and pushed it from her shoulders. A shiver rushed over her as the cool evening air caressed the exposed skin her tank top didn't cover. Her hands sat at her sides, trapped by her jacket sleeves. She could have pulled free, but she didn't want to. She wanted to be at his mercy, wanted to let him do what he would and see what followed.

Her core tightened in anticipation as he slid the spaghetti straps of her tank top down to her elbows, tugging her shirt with them. Her red bra lifted her breasts, exposing the top swells to him.

Kade leaned forward and kissed the valley between. He moved to the top of one breast, kissed her, then drew his tongue along the edge of her bra, sending a frisson of shivers through her. He seemed in no hurry, either, and his attention was so sensually sweet, she thought she might shatter in anticipation.

He caught her gaze, watching her with wonder and a hint of naughtiness. A sexy smile turned his lips and caught fire in her heart. He held her gaze as he lifted a finger and tugged down the edge of her bra.

She sucked in a breath as her breast came free of its constraint, and he glanced down.

"Damn, sweetheart." He cupped her from beneath. Her nipple contracted, the sensation achingly sweet, and she closed her eyes as he lowered his head.

"Good God," she whispered as he drew her inside, sucking her until every muscle tightened with need.

He reached behind her as he suckled her and undid the clasp on her bra, tugging it down with the rest of her clothes. Shadows played over his face as he cupped both of her breasts, massaging one while he made love to the other.

She pulled her hands free then, needing to feel him, to touch him. He released her, and she grasped the bottom of his shirt and pulled it upward. He assisted her, tugging it over his head and tossing it aside.

Afterward, she spread her hands as she covered his pecs, delighting in the power that rested beneath her touch. She drew her fingers up and over his strong shoulders, his skin smooth and heated despite the chill in the air.

She bent forward and kissed him on the curve between his shoulder and neck as he tightened his hold on her, forcing her nipples to graze his chest.

He groaned and slid his hands to her ass, molding her tighter against his erection. Proof of his desire taunted her, driving her need higher.

Then he fumbled with the button on her jeans, her waist-band growing slack as he met with success. He dipped his big hands down the back of her pants, slipping beneath her panties until he was flesh on flesh. He curled his blunt fingers into her skin, his touch demanding and seductive.

She lifted from him, getting to her knees, holding his head as she gazed down upon him. She lowered her head for a slow, possessive kiss, needing to show him exactly how much she wanted him.

"I think it's time to find a better position again," she said breathlessly.

He laughed. "You're right."

She moved from him, onto the sleeping bag, but he didn't let her go far. He removed her shoes and drew her jeans down her legs, leaving her with nothing but her red lacy panties.

Slowly, he lifted his gaze to hers. "I'm a lucky man, Noelle."

She smiled as heated lust whipped through her. "You should lose the rest of your clothes and get over here."

"Yes, ma'am." His boots, jeans, and boxer shorts joined the growing pile of clothes within a few blinks.

His body was beautiful. All angles and muscles, and she shivered at the thought of him making love with her.

She got to her knees, eager to touch him. "Come here."

He met her halfway, kissing her, before he lowered her to the sleeping bag.

"Goddamn," he whispered as he slid next to her. "You feel so good."

He covered her with his magnificent body, and she wrapped her arms and legs around him as the hard length of him settled against her. She shifted, bringing him to her entrance.

"Damn it," he whispered beneath his breath as he pulled from her embrace. "I forgot to put on a condom."

"Oh, no." She laughed. "I should have thought of that, should have said something."

He groped through their clothes and lifted his pants. "No worries. This will only take a second."

A chilly breeze nipped at her bare body, and she tugged one of the sleeping bags out from beneath her, holding it open until he returned to her.

"Are you cold?" he asked, pulling the cover over them.

"Not now that you're sharing your heat," she teased.

"I'm going to share more than that." He settled between her

legs and adjusted himself at her entrance. "Now, where were we?"

"You were about to make my night."

"Oh, yeah?" He pinned her arms over her head as he slid in the slightest bit. "What if I don't?"

She lifted beneath him, trying to draw him in farther. "You will. You can't resist."

His chuckle was deep and rich. "You're right. I can't."

He kissed her hard, stealing any thoughts she had beyond him and this moment. When she broke the kiss for air, he gripped her and buried himself inside her.

He hissed with pleasure as he drew out and filled her again. "Ah, sweetheart..."

She gripped him, holding him tight within her embrace as he plundered her. Everything inside her had turned to hot sensation as he loved her.

Desire built. Spread through her and then contracted, over and over again, until she thought she might scream.

Kade. Oh, God... "*Kade*." The tremor hit her low, stealing what breath she had as the exquisite sensation ripped through her.

He didn't stop, didn't give her a moment to compose herself, but sent her racing for the next thrill. Already mid-orgasm, she caught the updraft and raced toward another explosion of pleasure.

She lost count of how many times she'd called his name, how many times she'd contracted around him and had fallen off the delicious precipice. When he finally came, pumping his desire into her with a breathless curse, she could do nothing but smile.

Her limbs were weak, and he'd satiated her beyond explanation.

Kade collapsed on top of her, his thundering heart

pounding against her chest. They'd lost their cover, but she didn't care. The cool breeze felt wonderful on her heated body.

"Damn, Noelle," he whispered as he rolled and pulled her on top of him. "I don't want to sound cliché, but that was...amazing."

"*You* were amazing."

He laughed. "That's good, because it's been a while for me."

Darkness had settled around them, and she felt more than saw him. "Could have fooled me." She drew a hand over his chest, tracing his nipple with her finger. Euphoria owned her heart and soul, and she prayed the moment would linger forever.

He captured her hand and held it against his heart. "I needed to get my shit together before I thought about another relationship."

"She hurt you," Noelle whispered.

He turned and pushed her down on the makeshift bed before he laid his hard body over her. "Everything hurt back then. But as you said, that's in the past. It has no place here now. The only thing I want to think about is you."

He cupped her breast and sucked a nipple into his hot mouth. Despite her ability to believe it, her core contracted, igniting a slow ache. "Kade."

He answered with a mumble, not releasing her breast.

She laughed. She couldn't believe he'd want her again so soon, but she could feel his erection growing against her leg. "I'm not sure I can handle you again," she teased.

"I think you'll handle me just fine," he said, his voice finding her in the inky night. He drew a finger along her wet folds, and she shuddered. "Yes," he whispered, before he shifted and thrust inside her again.

Her back bowed as she arched upward to accommodate him. He stretched her, the feel of him inside her excruciatingly sensual, but she couldn't get enough. She wanted more. Needed more. And knew if he ever left her, she'd never be the same.

————

An hour later, Kade pulled Noelle into his arms. "I brought you all this way, and you haven't seen any stars."

The way he held her made her feel as if she was the most precious thing. "Oh, trust me. I've seen stars." The best kind of stars, started by desire and fueled by love.

His laugh rumbled in his chest. "You're so good for me."

A knot formed in her throat, and she hugged him instead of speaking. It was much too soon to fall for him, and she was desperately afraid of what would happen if he realized she'd already traveled down that slippery slope.

"Are you okay to stay and watch the stars for a while?" he asked. "You're not too cold?"

"I'm good," she whispered. She'd stay in his arms as long as he'd hold her.

15

The theater had been more than wonderful, and Noelle and Kade had made a standing date after the six weeks of auto mechanics classes ended. Instead of meeting at the school, she brought dinner and her car to his house, where they holed up inside his large garage. The end of October neared, bringing with it cold temperatures and the promise of snow.

Noelle didn't mind. She had a hot, handsome man to keep her warm.

She hadn't been able to get him out of her mind that entire day. They'd had other dates, had made passionate love several times over, but she treasured the quiet moments in his garage when it was just the two of them.

She pulled inside his garage, parking in the spot he'd cleared for her car. Kade was already there, tinkering with something at his workbench. He looked up, and a devastating grin curved his lips as he locked gazes with her. He wore his ball cap backward. Together with his ripped jeans and grease-stained t-shirt, she'd never seen anything sexier.

One look was all it took to send her thoughts and emotions

tumbling into a wild and happy frenzy. All the other moments of her day paled compared to the time she spent with him.

He opened her car door and loud rock music greeted her, like always, lightening her mood despite what kind of day she may have had.

She took his hand and allowed him to pull her into a heated embrace. The man was more potent than the Death Wish coffee she'd tried in Salt Lake, and far more addicting than her iced cinnamon rolls.

He captured her mouth, and she wondered if he realized how even the smallest touch, the lightest kiss, affected her.

Then he grinned as he pulled away, and she knew that he knew.

Kade studied her. "Hey, beautiful. I've been waiting for you."

Noelle narrowed her eyes into a teasing gaze. "You only want me for my soup and my car."

He touched the tip of her nose. "You've got that right."

Kade closed the garage door, blocking out the blustery winds. Then he took the brown paper sack from her backseat and carried it to the little table he'd erected a few weeks ago. Originally, they'd eaten in the house, but she liked his garage, the place where he enjoyed his passion, where he most wanted to spend his free time.

He'd invited her into his sanctuary, where Ian had never made her feel welcome when he took off on his motorcycle for a ride with the boys. Not that she begrudged him time with his friends, but he always seemed more excited to go with them than stay with her.

Kade removed the soup container and lifted the lid. "Looks like we're eating chicken noodle and playing under your hood tonight. Two of my favorite things."

She rolled her eyes at his pun, although she did intend to go home satisfied. "Good thing I like you."

He caught her around the waist and pulled her to him for a scorching kiss. "Damn good thing."

Noelle arched her brow. "If you don't stop kissing me like that, we'll be eating cold soup."

"Really?" He lifted his brows, a naughty smile on his lips. "Because I kind of like cold soup."

She smiled and scoffed. "No, you don't."

He popped the button on her jeans. "I do now."

Oh hell.

He had her zipper down when his phone rang. "Uh-uh," he mumbled toward the interruption as he kissed her neck and tugged down her jeans.

Her focus flipped from the spot where his lips touched her to the feel of him slipping his hand down her panties and into her slick folds. She gasped as he grazed her sensitive nub.

"Kade," she whispered, as their surroundings faded to a sultry haze.

The ringing quieted as he removed her jeans and panties at the same time, his hands touching and teasing. It took nothing for him to set her on fire. Liquid desire pooled at her center, and she waited for the moment he'd touch her again. He opened his fly, and the rock hard length of him sprung from his boxers.

She wrapped her fingers around him, moving her hand over his shaft, enjoying the power that rested there. "Are you going to give this to me?" she teased.

Something dark and seductive flared in his eyes. "Damn right. I'm going to give it to you right here, right now."

Danger swirled in the air between them, and she quivered, eager for him to fulfill his promise.

She glanced around the room, wondering about his intentions as he backed her toward her car. Cool metal met the slice of exposed skin on her back, and she shivered.

When he spoke, his voice was low and sexy. "I've thought about taking you here like this, bent over your car, so many times."

The moisture in her mouth evaporated.

He pulled her sweater over her head in one quick move. He didn't pause as he undid her black bra and tossed it behind him, leaving her bare to his gaze.

She couldn't take her eyes from his. This sexy, alpha side of him thrilled her, and maybe scared her a little, too.

"Yes," he said as he turned her so her back faced him, and he took her breasts with rough hands. He massaged her mounds and pinched her nipples until she gasped with pleasure. She reached over her shoulder and caressed his jaw, then his lips.

He nipped her fingers hard enough to send a shiver coursing through her. She sucked in a breath, and he slowly lowered one hand down her body, over her stomach, inching his way toward her most sensitive areas.

She arched, knowing where he headed, wishing he wouldn't tease her so.

He pulled her panties from her with rough, demanding hands, and then pushed her forward until he bent her over the hood of her car. Cold metal kissed her nipples as his feverish hands caressed her ass.

Her breaths came heavy, uneven as anticipation toyed with her. "Kade," she begged, caught up in his fantasy.

Wild and wanton feelings, almost feral, owned her and seemed to steal her civility. "Take me now," she whispered as she curled her hands into fists and lifted her ass higher into the air. If he didn't, she'd certainly die.

"Hell, yes," he growled. He slammed into her with a force

that rocked her world. Need combusted into fiery sensation, and she cried out, surprised he'd taken her so quickly.

He held her hips as he pumped into her over and over. The ringing of his cell phone caused him to lose his rhythm, but he quickly caught it again.

Intense passion stole all sense of time. At some point, she gasped as she shuddered around him again. He stiffened, holding her tightly against him as he gave a few more jerky pumps, and then collapsed on top of her.

He lay there for a moment, his head on her back, their heavy breaths mixing with the rock music. Slowly, he ran his hands over her sides and then turned her, pulling her into his arms. He tilted her chin, and she gazed up into his dreamy brown eyes.

"You are the sexiest, sweetest thing I've ever encountered." He kissed her on the lips. "I can't get enough of you."

"And you still have all your clothes on." While she was butt naked.

He chuckled. "Sorry. Fantasy of mine."

She shook her head in mock disapproval, but smiled.

His phone rang again, and he sighed and pulled it from his pocket. "It's my sister. I'd better answer."

"Krystal?"

He shook his head as he tapped his phone's screen, tucked it between his shoulder and ear, and bent to retrieve her clothes. "Hi Kaitlin," he said, wiggling his brows as he held out her lacy bra.

Noelle tried to snatch it, but he held it out as though he would help her put it on.

She rolled her eyes, but slid her hands through the armholes.

"She what?" he said, his voice taking on a serious note as he fastened her bra.

Noelle turned to see Kade's face, but he stepped away from

her, preoccupied by his phone conversation. Whatever it was, it didn't seem to be good news.

She quickly donned the rest of her clothes as he cussed under his breath and asked vague questions.

Kade gave Noelle a brief glance. "Yeah. I can come."

Then he blew out a breath. "No, I don't want Dad to handle it. I'll leave right now."

He ended the call and turned to Noelle. "I'm so sorry. I have to head into Pinecone. A family problem of sorts."

"Want me to come with?" She really wanted to meet the rest of his family.

He suddenly seemed exhausted. "No. I might be awhile. I'll explain when I have more time."

"Okay." She glanced around, disappointed that their lovely evening had come to a screeching halt. "You keep the soup. You can eat it later."

"No, you take it. I'll grab something at my parents." He picked up the bag and handed it to her as he escorted her to her car.

"What's wrong, Kade?" Whatever his sister said had visibly upset him, and she wanted to help. "What can I do?"

"You can't do anything. I'm not sure anyone can. Just...let me deal with this now, and I promise I'll make it up to you. I'll call you tomorrow."

What could she say? He obviously wanted her to leave so he could, and she stood in his way. "Okay." She kissed him, but the gesture seemed to be lost on his lips.

Tendrils of fear plucked at her, but she refused to give them any weight. She put a hand on his cheek and waited until he fully focused on her. Once again, her heart prompted her to tell him the depth of her emotions, but she didn't have the courage. "Drive safe. I'll see you in the morning. Coffee, okay?"

A flash of gratitude curved his lips, and it reassured her that this time, he seemed to see her. "Thanks for understanding."

She nodded and gave him another quick kiss, wishing her mouth could linger on his for a while longer. "Bye," she said and climbed into her car.

She found it difficult to leave, sensing something was wrong, wishing she could force him to tell her. But she had to trust him, so she would. When it was time, he'd tell her.

———

The drive to his parents' home in Pinecone might have been the longest ever. Kade feared what waited for him at the other end. Dreaded the almost certain confrontation. Needed desperately to put the past behind him.

The sick feeling churning in his stomach compounded when he turned into his parents' long drive and his headlights illuminated the little red Honda parked behind his mom's sedan.

Hillary.

He sucked in a breath and turned off the engine. Brisk fall air slapped him as he stepped onto the gravel drive and shut the door. What on God's green earth would she want now, and what would he have to do to get rid of her?

He pulled open the screen and then the door, the familiar scents of home and family not comforting him as usual.

16

Kade found them in the usually cheerful kitchen, his parents sitting on one side of the table, while his ex-wife and his sister, Kaitlin, sat on the other. A worried look hovered on his mother's face, deepening the soft lines near her eyes, while his father's dark mustache couldn't hide the frown on his lips.

Hillary widened her eyes and smiled when he stepped into the room. "Kade." She stood and approached him. Her blue eyes seemed clear, and her blond hair swayed as she walked.

He hesitated, letting her erase the distance between them, wary of her intentions. The last time he'd seen her, she'd been strung out on meth and she'd ended up screaming at him uncontrollably. Tonight, she appeared to have showered and didn't seem high, but he couldn't be certain.

She held open her arms as she reached for him and wrapped them around his neck. "It's so good to see you."

He glanced at his parents over her shoulder. Neither seemed happy, though entertained interest held in Kaitlin's eyes. He frowned at her.

"It's good to see you, too," he lied as he disengaged himself from her embrace. "Why are you here, Hillary?"

"I'm sorry for forcing your hand." She glanced guiltily at his parents. "I know they were trying to protect you when they wouldn't let me know where you were. But I really needed to see you."

He took her by the elbow and steered her toward the front door. "Let's go outside where we can talk in private." She was his problem, not his family's. He'd deal with her. Plus, he didn't need Kaitlin to overhear everything and blab to the rest of his sisters.

He braced himself as he dropped to the porch swing, the overhead light casting a yellow circle around them. The sweet scent of perfume reached out to him, and he recognized the fragrance she'd always worn during the first years of their marriage. He had to admit she looked good, looked like the woman who'd stolen his heart.

"I really am sorry, Kade. It's not like me to force my way in."

It wasn't like the old Hillary, but who knew these days? "Is there something I can help you with?"

She released a weighted sigh. "I came to apologize."

That surprised him. "Apologize?"

She gave an embarrassed laugh. "Don't seem so shocked."

Kade widened his eyes and stared down at his boots. He hadn't expected this day to arrive, ever. He'd made his peace with the demons of their past and would have been content to leave things alone.

She shifted on the swing, but kept to her side. "I don't expect you to care, but I wanted you to know I've joined a twelve-step program. I've been doing well, getting better. My counselor says I'm making great progress, and I feel like I am. I feel like the person I used to be."

They'd both lost their innocence, their faith, and their

marriage when their baby had died. "Neither of us are the people we used to be."

"I know," she said softly. "We endured something no one should have to."

"I'm not sure endured is the correct word." He'd suffered. She'd checked out.

She put a hand on his forearm, and he flashed his gaze to her, suspicion raising the alarm. But her look was remorseful and sincere. "I can't ask for your forgiveness, Kade. I don't deserve it."

He couldn't argue with that.

"I want to say that I wish I could have been as strong as you were, but I wasn't. Losing...Sara..." She paused, and he watched her throat work over a swallow. "Losing Sara was more than I could handle. You deserved a wife that could stand with you during those hard times. The alcohol and the drugs killed the pain, and for a short while, it was such a blessed relief not to see her little face every moment of the day, not to feel that aching emptiness."

"And the men?" He shouldn't have thrown that in her face. It made no difference now. But it still killed him to know she sought solace with someone else.

"Yes," she said, looking down in shame. It was the first time she hadn't denied what she'd done, so maybe she was making progress. "I can't explain them. I hated myself so much at that point and knew you deserved someone better. I can't tell you if I was too drunk to consider the consequences or if I'd hoped it would chase you away because I was such a failure."

"Well, that part of it certainly worked."

He hadn't wanted to believe she could do such a thing, not the woman he'd known since they'd been kids, not the woman he'd given his virginity to, not the woman he'd married. He'd lived in denial and let her cheat for months before he'd finally walked. He'd tried to understand, tried to get her help until he could no longer ignore the harsh reality that he'd lost everything.

She met his gaze. "You'll never know how sorry I am that I let you down."

His own throat closed with emotion. He'd made it through that dark alley of pain and didn't want to travel it again. It took him several moments to lasso the devastating memories she'd released, to bury them again. "I'm glad you could finally get help."

Unshed tears glittered in her eyes. "Me, too."

"I wanted to help you, Hillary." His voice trembled with unwanted emotion. "I did everything I could."

"I know," she said, her own voice teary. "I was too lost back then."

He nodded and wiped the moisture from his eyes. Then he sniffed and stood. "Thank you for the apology. I appreciate it."

She followed him up and met his gaze with searching eyes. "Thank you for accepting it. I know coming here is part of my recovery, but I've wanted to say these things to you for a while now. We once shared a life, and I owe it to those two people that we were to give this a better ending."

He nodded. "Yeah."

"I should go. I'm sure I've upset your parents enough already." She put her arms around him again, and he responded by giving her a quick, awkward hug. "Goodnight, Kade."

"Goodnight, Hillary."

She walked down the steps, seeming a little lost in their big world, but standing on her own two feet. He could feel gratitude for that, and he prayed she'd continue on her path to wellness. He no longer had to wonder if he'd see her face on the television news, her body found in some ditch, left there by whoever had given her too many drugs.

17

Noelle packed two cup carriers full of coffee and loaded a bag with doughnuts and other goodies. "I'll be right back," she hollered to April in the backroom.

She pushed open the front door with her butt and headed toward the newly constructed motel next to Rumors. Kade hadn't been in for his early morning coffee yet, and she grew tired of waiting. She wanted to give him his space, but she cared about him and needed to know he was okay.

Weak morning light filtered over the quiet town, and her breath frosted lightly in front of her. The latter days of fall had come much too fast, and it wouldn't be long before the holidays would be upon them.

When she reached Kade's motel, she carefully stacked one layer of coffee cups on top of the other and slowly opened the door, careful not to disturb her load. One of the construction workers caught her plight and rushed to help her, carrying one of the cup carriers along with the bag of goodies to the front counter.

"Thanks, Noelle." Edgar opened the bag and peered inside.

"Can I sneak away with the whole thing?" The burly construction worker looked at her with hopeful eyes.

Noelle laughed. "If you think you can get away with it."

"That's not going to happen," Kade said as he turned the corner and joined them. "Mmm...I knew it was your coffee I smelled."

He slipped a hand around her waist and tugged her against him as though she belonged there. "This is a nice surprise."

She soaked up the feel of Kade next to her. "I wondered if you and the guys could use a little caffeine this morning to wake you up and chase away the chill."

"It's definitely nippy out there," Edgar said. He pulled two doughnuts from the bag and snagged a cup of coffee. "I'm taking two 'cause I'm the only one working around here this morning. The rest of these guys are lazy sons-of-bitches." He winked as he shoved two-thirds of one doughnut into his mouth and headed back to where he worked on the electrical switches behind the front desk.

Kade pulled her into his arms and smiled down at her. "Good morning, sweetheart."

Warmth and attraction bubbled inside her. "Good morning."

He placed his lips over hers, his kiss soft, then growing more heated. Noelle pulled away before Edgar got too excited by their public display of affection.

"What?" Kade asked under his breath.

She directed her gaze in an exaggerated way toward Edgar.

"Don't worry about him. I'm sure Edgar has kissed his share of women."

Edgar pretended to cough. "Don't tell my wife that."

The three of them laughed, and Noelle found it hard to reconcile that Kade had deserted her the previous evening to run off and handle a family emergency.

She slipped a coffee from the container and handed it to Kade. "Black like you like it."

"I'd say you know me too well, but I think you know me just right." He took a sip. "Perfect."

She smiled, happy that she could please him. "I worried about you last night," she said in a lowered voice.

"You didn't need to." He took her hand. "Come on. Let's go tell the others you've brought coffee."

"What happened?" she asked. He seemed fine now, but not so much last night.

"I'll tell you later," he whispered as he tugged on her hand. "When we're alone."

"Don't be sneaking off to the laundry room," Edgar called after them.

"That's not a bad idea," Kade tossed back. "If you don't see me for a while, you'll know I'm busy."

"Ah, hell," Edgar responded. "Here I was satisfied with my coffee."

Noelle shook her head, a faint blush heating her cheeks. She'd been around enough guys and their sexual banter that she shouldn't have cared, but for some reason having Edgar voice her thoughts left her heated.

Kade led the way down the main hall and stopped inside what really was the laundry room. He set his coffee on a side counter and lifted the radio that rested there. "Hey, y'all," he said to the device. "Noelle brought breakfast. It's waiting at the front desk."

He kicked the door closed behind him and advanced on her, a confident man intent upon his desire.

Noelle laughed and backed away from Kade until she bumped into a wall behind her. "Edgar was only kidding." She held out her hands as though to keep him away, but there was nothing that could keep him from her heart.

He pressed into her until his hard body connected with hers in the most delicious way. "*I'm* not kidding."

It surprised her still, how his closeness could steal her breath. Her sanity.

Kade cupped her face and studied her. "You have the most amazing eyes. Like a brilliant sky on a summer day."

She blinked and then grinned.

"What?" he asked softly, tracing the curves of her mouth with his gaze.

"I didn't realize you were a poet."

His forefinger replaced his gaze, and his touch sent a shiver through her. "I'm trying to seduce you. Not make you laugh."

"Oh," she said, her smile growing bigger. "I'll try to be serious then."

"Right." He took both her hands and slid them up the wall over her head, leaving her vulnerable to him. "Maybe this will help."

He lowered his lips to hers in a crushing kiss. She fought to remember where she was through the haze that consumed her.

"Kade," she whispered against his mouth, between kisses. "There are people everywhere here."

He kissed across her jaw to the sweet spot beneath her ear. "So..."

Heated tingles spiked through her. "So, we can't do this here." Even to her own ears, she sounded breathless, wanton.

"Who says?" He released a hand to cup her breast, and she took the opportunity to take his jaw, forcing him to look at her. Hazy lust filled his orbs, making her ache to lose herself in them as well. It would be so easy...

"I have to get back. April's starting on the lunch menu and can't man the counter, too."

He growled and captured her hand again, holding her in place. "The only way I'll let you go is if I can see you tonight."

That was exactly what she wanted to hear. "Your place? Usual time?"

He shook his head. "Nah, I need to take you out, show you off."

She laughed. "You're in an awfully good mood today."

"Yeah." He grinned. "Life has been treating me pretty damn good lately, and it's only going to get better."

Hints at a future with him stirred her happiness until it bubbled over. She slid from his grasp and captured his face. "For me, too."

He kissed her long and slow, leaving her with a heady feeling she couldn't remember experiencing.

"Good," he said softly. "You deserve it. We both do."

She hugged him tightly to her and gave him another quick kiss. "I'll see you later?"

"Yes. I'll meet you at your house about an hour after you leave work."

"I'll be waiting for you." She hated to leave him, but couldn't wait for later. She left him in the laundry room, hoping he'd have as difficult of a time working as she would.

"Bye, Edgar," she said, as she headed for the front door.

"That was fast," he said with a laugh. "If you want a real man, you come talk to me."

Noelle rolled her eyes and shook her head. She was about to reach for the door to push it open when a woman came strolling through. She had gorgeous blond hair and the bluest eyes Noelle had ever seen.

"Hi," the woman said with a smile. "Do you know where I might find Kade?"

Noelle turned to Edgar, and he lifted his brows. "It's okay, Noelle. I'll go get him."

The woman glanced awkwardly between her and Edgar. "Sorry, I didn't mean to interrupt."

"No problem. I was on my way out," Noelle said with a smile, deciding she must be Kade's caterer. The grand opening drew nearer, and she was sure they'd have things to discuss.

As Noelle stepped onto the sidewalk, her heart expanded. She couldn't have asked for a better morning.

———

Kade grinned as he lifted another screw and drilled it into the drywall for shelving. He enjoyed working with his hands, enjoyed that he could use his skills to create and build. His motel in Pinecone had already been built when he'd acquired it, and he loved the business side of that, too. But this...helping to build his business from the ground up brought him immense satisfaction.

And Noelle. Having her near inspired similar feelings of excitement and contentment. Life was better with her around.

Kade grabbed a screw and lined it up, but dropped it when he tried to settle the drill on its head. He bent to retrieve it, the hairs on his arms stiffening as he straightened. He glanced over his shoulder, and the sight of his ex-wife startled him. "Hillary? What are you doing here?"

Things had gone so well the previous night, and he'd finally shed the gloom that had hung over him. They'd made their peace. They could both move on.

The sight of her in Aspen brought back the doubt.

She sighed and gave him an embarrassed smile. "Sorry. I would have called, but you changed your number."

To escape her endless drunken rants. "What can I help you with?"

She stepped into the room and leaned against the door-jamb. She wore her hair down, soft curls falling over her green blouse. This was the woman he remembered, the woman she should have always been. "I wanted to thank you for last night, for the civil discussion."

"You're welcome. Contrary to what you might have thought, I never wanted us to be enemies."

"I know. Our problems were entirely my fault. I wish I could go back to the way things were. Wish I could have made different choices. My counselor says I did the best I could with what I had and that my past doesn't make my future."

He nodded. "Wise words."

"I miss us." Her blunt reply hit deep in his heart.

He studied her for a moment, unsure how to respond. "Me, too. We both got the rotten end of a deal."

She smiled. "Remember when we used to sneak out at night, back when we were in high school? We'd head down to the river to swim, to make love, and then we'd lay there and watch the stars?"

His emotions tightened, a knee-jerk response to the pain he'd endured. "I remember."

She sighed. "We should drive out there, for old time's sake, and look around."

He realized then where she was headed, and her purpose for seeking him out. "I don't think so, Hillary."

She tilted her head, the movement sending a waft of her familiar perfume into the air. "Why not?"

It was tempting to try to go back and recapture what had died, but that wouldn't work. They couldn't erase the ugliness that had brought them to this point. "I'm seeing someone."

Someone who brightened his day. Someone who lightened his load.

Someone he wanted in his future.

Her breath rushed out of her. "Oh. I was afraid of that." She blinked a few times and then met his gaze. "Is it serious?"

He shrugged. "Maybe." He and Noelle hadn't voiced their

thoughts or hopes, but there was certainly something between them.

"Just *maybe?*" She raised a hopeful brow.

He shifted, uncomfortable with the direction of their conversation. He didn't want to hurt her, didn't want to derail her recovery, but he couldn't encourage her either. "We had our chance, Hillary. It didn't work."

"It did, though. For a long, long time. Who can better understand what you've gone through? We can help each other heal."

"I don't need help healing. I'm good."

"Have you talked to someone about it? If you bury your feelings like you've always done, they're going to resurface down the road."

He released a breath, recognizing she was stirring trouble. "I don't need to talk to anyone. I've dealt with things in my own way."

She gave him a doubtful look, but smiled. "I won't push. I'm just grateful we're talking again. Know that I'm here if you need me."

He wanted to take her and shove her out the door, and yell at her to get the hell out of his life. But he didn't.

"Thanks." He held up the drill. "I should get back to work now."

"Of course. This place is beautiful. Congratulations."

He nodded and then waited. She glanced around the room and then approached him, giving him another awkward hug. "I'll see you later."

He didn't respond as she turned to leave. He didn't want to see her later. As cruel as it sounded, he'd be happy if he never saw her again.

————

Noelle handed the cup of coffee to Wayne Staker. "Here you go. Tell Nancy I said hi."

The Aspen resident often came across as gruff, but since he'd retired, he seemed much happier. "Will do. You have a nice day."

The older man smiled, the wrinkles near his eyes crinkling, and Noelle returned the smile to keep her jaw from falling open. He'd always been civil to her, but never downright cordial.

"You, too." She shook her head as he left, life never failing to surprise her.

Before she could return to the backroom, the bell on the door jingled again, and Kade's caterer walked in.

"Good morning," Noelle said in greeting.

"Hello again." The woman smiled, and Noelle liked her right away.

"I was hoping for a cup of coffee and something yummy before I make the drive back to Pinecone. I think I'll have one of those gooey cinnamon rolls. It will totally mess with my diet, but I'm sort of celebrating today."

"Then, by all means." Noelle slid the roll onto a disposable plate and set it on the counter before she filled a cup with coffee.

"Are you celebrating something fun?" Noelle asked as she placed the lid on top of the coffee cup.

The woman tilted her head from side to side as though she wasn't sure. "I've just recently reconnected with my ex-husband. You probably know him. He's building the motel next door."

18

For an eternal moment, Noelle's world froze. *Not again.* Then nausea climbed her throat. She glanced down at the credit card the woman had handed to her and then slid it through her machine. Hillary Collier.

She swallowed and handed the card back to Kade's ex-wife, using slow, meticulous movements to keep the woman from noticing her world crashing around her. "I do know him. You say you're getting back together?"

"It's still tentative, but I have a good feeling about it. We hit a rough patch awhile back." A sad look fell over her face. "We lost a child, and it's taken us both time to move beyond it. But I hope now that time has passed, we can revive what we lost. I still love him, and I know he loves me, too."

Hillary slipped her card into her wallet and gave a soft laugh. "Except for the past year and a half, he and I have been inseparable since we were fourteen. We had so many good years together. It's hard to let that go, you know? Plus, he needs me. He hasn't grieved for our child, hasn't shed a tear, so I know the grief is still stuck inside him, and I'm the right person to help him."

Noelle nodded. Thankfully, the numbness had taken over.

"I had some tough months that are a blur for me, but before that, I can't really remember life without him. We owe it to ourselves to give it another shot, don't you agree?"

What could she say? "I would if I were in your shoes." And Noelle stood in their way. Unless Kade had already decided to break things off. Though he didn't seem like it that morning. But maybe things had changed since Hillary had visited him.

Oh, God. She was going to be sick.

"Thanks for this." Kade's ex-wife held up her coffee and roll. "I'm sure I'll be seeing much more of you. He's made Aspen his home, so I'm certain I'll end up here, too. It's lovely, you know, with the quiet streets and friendly people. I think I could like it here."

Noelle nodded and then turned, leaving the woman at the counter. She headed into the backroom where April sliced bread for sandwiches. She placed a steadying hand against the wall and inhaled through the sharp, stabbing pains. "I need to go."

April glanced up, her expression switching from questioning to concern. "Are you okay?" She left the loaf on the cutting board and approached Noelle. "Your face is pure white."

Noelle shook her head, unable to speak. Tears gathered and then fell.

"*Noelle.*" She grasped her hand. "What's wrong? What happened?"

"Kade." Her voice cracked. "His ex-wife wants to work things out."

April's expression dropped. "No. Is that what he told you?"

"She told me. She wants him back, and she thinks they have a chance."

April narrowed her gaze, looking uncertain. "What does Kade say?"

"I don't know." Her words ended in a sob. "I don't want to

know. If there's a chance for them, how can I stand in their way? If he doesn't try, then he'll regret it forever, and I don't want to be his regret."

She crumpled onto April's shoulder, her heart erupting with raw, exposed pain. She wanted a man for herself, not someone who belonged to another. She wanted his whole heart. A heart that belonged to only her.

"I'm sorry." April rubbed her back and then snagged a tissue for her.

"I can't be here today." She needed to escape before her soul completely combusted. She needed air and a quiet place to think...and, oh God, how would she face the next minute?

"Go. I can handle things here. Do what you need to feel better. I'll call you later, okay?"

Noelle nodded. She gathered her purse and coat, and then she stumbled outside, heading toward her car. She couldn't look at Kade's place, couldn't think about what life would be like with their businesses right next to each other.

———

Kade smiled when he pulled into Noelle's drive just before six. The setting sun shone golden on her as she sat on her front porch step waiting for him. Red and yellow leaves lay scattered on the ground around her, and he took a moment to store the beautiful image in his mind.

He exited his truck with a smile in his heart, but as he neared her, something changed. Maybe it was the slump of her shoulders or the haunted look in her eyes.

"What's wrong?" he said, holding out his hands to pull her to her feet.

She stared, tears gathering in her already-red eyes.

"Noelle," he said as panic overtook him.

She blinked a few times, then grabbed the handrail and stood. "This isn't going to work."

Her words were a sucker punch to his gut, and he fought to straighten his scrambled thoughts. "What?" That was the last thing he'd expected to hear.

She struggled to keep from crying. He wanted so much to reach out to her to comfort her, but she'd thrown a wall between them. "This thing between us, whatever it is, we have to stop."

"Jesus, Noelle. You're not making sense." He wanted to think it was a joke, but the look on her face told him otherwise. "Why would you say that?"

She covered her mouth for a moment before she spoke. "I talked to your wife today."

Anger unfurled inside him. What had Hillary done? "I don't have a wife."

"Ex-wife then, but she believes you're getting back together."

"We're not getting back together." He reached for her then, but she moved away, up another step. "Why would you listen to her, Noelle?"

Her bottom lip trembled. "She still loves you. You were together for a long, long time, have a ton of history together."

"That doesn't change the fact that we *are* divorced."

She wiped the tears from her eyes and focused on him with an intense stare. "If your baby hadn't died, would you still be together?"

"Hell, Noelle. I don't know." He practically shouted the words at her. He understood the direction her thoughts had taken, but she was wrong. "How can anyone predict the future?"

She glanced down at her feet, pain radiating from her expression.

"Just stop Noelle," he whispered, fear kicking in. "Don't do this."

"She said you haven't grieved your loss yet. She said she loves you and wants to help you. I can't stand in the way of that." Her words ended in a sob. "The two of you belong together."

"*No—*"

"I can't invest anymore, Kade. Not with a man who doesn't belong to me."

Frustration tore at him. "You're not listening to me. You're not hearing what I'm telling you."

"I don't need to. I saw it in her face. That thing I've always longed for. She loves you. She wants you back. It's only a matter of time before you realize you need to find out whether things could work between you again. I can't be here when that happens." She placed a hand over her heart. "I can't take it."

"So, you're going to listen to everyone else but me? You're going to dump me because someone else wants me? You must not think a hell of a lot about me if you're willing to let me go so easily."

She bit her bottom lip, but didn't respond.

"*Fuck.*" He shook his head. "This isn't about Hillary at all, is it? God, Noelle, if you want out, then just say it. You don't need to drag up all this shit from my past and throw it in my face. If you're too spineless to tell me how you really feel, then fine, blame it on me."

He stared at her, praying she'd stop his tirade, praying she'd believe what he said. She remained silent, letting his words lash at her.

"Fine. I'll be the prick who used you and dumped you when my ex-wife came back to town. You can tell everyone I'm a bastard, and they'll never need to know you're a coward."

He turned and stomped halfway to his truck before pausing. "I'm so fucking over this shit." He growled and punched the air.

Inside his truck, he fired up the engine and tore out of her gravel drive, spraying rock everywhere to ease his shredded heart.

———

Noelle dropped back onto the porch as Kade sped away. Her heart gathered inward on itself with a crushing pressure, and several moments passed before she could breathe again. She didn't bother stopping her tears. Let them rain. Maybe they would clear away some of the overwhelming pain that washed her insides like acid.

The only thing that kept her from feeling like the world's worst person was the knowledge that he *would* regret it if he didn't give his relationship with Hillary every chance. Noelle had to love him enough to let him go.

And love herself enough, too. She wanted a man who was wholly hers. Not the shell of someone desecrated by another.

This would be okay. She would survive.

She'd made this trek too many times before to forget the painful path that ultimately softened.

She hoped.

19

Kade pulled to the side of the road near Noelle's house, knowing he needed to calm down. He rolled down the windows and let the cool evening air blow through. Deep breaths. Think rationally.

None of this was okay with him.

Hillary had no right to insert herself into his life again. Despite what Noelle thought, the love that had once existed between him and his ex was dead. Cold, buried in the ground, along with their daughter.

The statement didn't make him mean or cruel. It was just a fact.

One he intended to make clear immediately.

———

Kade paused as he stood at the door of his ex-mother-in-law's house on the outskirts of Pinecone. He hadn't been certain he'd find Hillary there, had no idea where she'd been staying. But he'd guessed, and it had paid off.

He rang the doorbell and then rapped on the wood.

Hillary opened the door a few moments later. A warm smile quickly replaced her look of surprise. "*Kade*. Come in."

He gave her a stern look and then brushed past her. "This won't take long." He stopped inside the door and turned to her.

She closed it behind him and met his gaze. Her brows dipped as she caught on to his mood. "Is everything okay?"

"No, everything is not okay. I don't know *what the hell* you think you're doing, but you need to stay out of my life. You had no right to tell Noelle you wanted to get back together with me, no right to make her think there was a chance in hell of that ever happening. Now, she's certain that's the best thing for me, and she kicked me out of her life."

Hillary opened her mouth, then closed it, then gave a slight shake of her head. "Noelle?"

"The woman I'm in love with."

"I-I'm sorry. I don't know Noelle. I certainly didn't tell her anything. The only person I spoke to in Aspen today besides you was..." She widened her eyes. "Does she work at the coffee shop next door?"

He could see from her face she was genuinely shocked. "She owns Rumors."

Hillary turned and sagged against the end of the couch. "I'm so sorry, Kade. I didn't know." She lifted her gaze to him. "I had just left you and was feeling very hopeful about us. I didn't realize who she was. You said you were seeing someone, but it didn't seem serious. I feel like we owe it to ourselves to see who we are on this side of tragedy and if there's anything we can salvage to make us whole again."

The fire fizzled out of him. He sighed and leaned against the couch next to her. "You can't keep pushing this, Hillary. We're divorced."

"I know that, Kade, and I understand it. I would have divorced me, too. But things have changed again, for the better.

We've made it through the shadows to the other side. For our daughter's sake, don't you think we should try?"

He met her gaze directly. "I don't want to sound harsh, Hillary, but I need to be blunt here. What happened sucked. It destroyed us both. I don't think you realize, but when I finally let go of you, it was because something inside me had died. I had to let go, or the rest of me would have died, too."

"I can't go back," he continued. "No, I don't want to go back. I've rebuilt a life for me. It's been hard earned, and I deserve it. I deserve to be happy. What happened, our baby, our marriage will forever be a part of who I am, but if I try to go back, it would be like ripping my soul out all over again. I can't do it. I won't do it."

He exhaled a deep breath. "Do you understand?"

She nodded, a sad look on her face. "I'm sorry for how I hurt you."

He shrugged. "I'm sorry that's how we ended, too. *But it ended.* I hope me telling you this won't set you back on your path to recovery."

"It won't. I'm stronger now. I'd hoped, but..." She put a hand on his arm. "What about you? I worry you won't be okay. You must allow yourself to grieve her."

He snorted. "What makes you think I haven't?" He couldn't count the number of hours he'd cried, cussed, and begged God to make everything okay.

"Kaitlin."

"She told you that?" His sister never did know how to mind her own business.

"She's worried about you, too."

"Just because she didn't see it doesn't mean it didn't happen. You're going to have to take my word for that."

She sighed, a defeated look on her face. "Okay."

"I'm going to go now, Hillary. And I'm not looking back. I

encourage you to do the same. Go find a life where you can be happy. We owe it to ourselves."

She gave a slow nod. "Yes. I intend to do that."

He shook her hand, hoping once and for all he'd put his past to rest.

"She loves you, you know," Hillary said as he reached for the doorknob.

He turned back to her, a glimmer of hope striking deep in his heart. "How do you know? What did she say to you?"

"She didn't say anything, but she let you go. She loved you enough to let you go."

Damned if he wouldn't love her enough to get her back.

———

Noelle rolled into work the next morning, her head pounding like the jackhammers and nail guns she'd listened to for months while Kade had built next door to her. The insides of her eyelids felt as though they'd been dusted with sand, and her heart ached with desperate longing.

The emptiness that usually stepped in hours after a breakup had deserted her like the traitorous bitch she was. Noelle had changed her mind many times during the night, picking up her phone, prepared to beg for forgiveness so she wouldn't have to suffer. But before she could dial, her brain would remind her she didn't want to be selfish and have them both suffer for it later.

At some point, the numbness would have to kick in.

Noelle stepped from her car as the first vestiges of light peeked over the mountains. The days were getting shorter, and it promised to be a long, cold winter.

She dug her keys from her purse as she stepped onto the sidewalk in front of her shop, and then stopped as unfamiliar, shadowed objects caught her attention. She squinted in the dim light as she slowly moved forward.

They looked like...flowers. In metal containers lining the front of her building. Orange, red, and yellow mums and white daisies.

She glanced around her, but no one moved about in the early morning hours of the quiet town. Who would do that? Why?

Had April? To cheer her up?

But there were so many...

She lifted her keys to open the shop and then froze when she caught sight of an enormous heart painted on the glass of her front door. Someone had written *I love you* inside the symbol. *Only you.*

Her heart nudged her toward an obvious answer, but she shot it down. Seth must have a surprise for April. They'd been married in the fall. Maybe it was their anniversary, although it seemed like it had been closer to winter.

Still...

She slid the key into the lock.

Kade's voice came to her through the crisp morning air. "Noelle."

She inhaled a surprised breath and put a hand to her mouth. She couldn't move, couldn't turn around. What if she'd imagined his voice, and it wasn't real?

He touched her shoulder, and she broke.

She turned to him, caught the look of determination on his face.

"Did you read it?" he asked, his voice firm.

She nodded.

"It's true, Noelle. I love you. Only you."

"But—"

He covered her mouth with a hand, pushing her back until

she bumped against the door. "No. There are no buts. There's me and you, and no one else. You have my heart, and I want yours."

A rumble of emotions shook her core, and she stared at him in the weak light. *He was here. He said he loved her.*

Kade released her mouth, but didn't move away. "Give me your heart, Noelle," he demanded. "I want it and need it."

His voice softened, and he slid his knuckles down her cheek. "I know you're scared. I'm scared, too, but if you give me your heart, I promise to love it and protect it with every fiber of my being."

Tears trickled down her face as her throat squeezed tight with emotion.

"No." He wiped at the moisture. "Don't cry."

"I love you," she whispered as she threw her arms around his neck. "You've had my heart for a long time now."

Kade gave her a solemn nod. "I had it. I know I did, but you took it back."

She shook her head, a happy sob escaping her lips. "I wanted to, but I couldn't. It stayed with you."

He tilted his head back and grinned as though he'd won the lottery. Then he met her gaze, his shining with happiness. "I can't tell you how many times I've cursed God. The things he's put me through. Things I thought I wouldn't survive. But they all brought me here, to you. They've made me recognize what I have now, how precious and perfect it is. I love you, Noelle. If you'll have me, I'll stay with you forever."

Her heart exploded with joy. "I'll have you, Kade, and I'll keep you forever." She pressed her lips against his with a laugh.

He accepted her lighthearted kiss. Took it and turned it into something dangerously addictive, something she wanted for the rest of her life.

"We should take this inside," he mumbled against her lips.

"We should." She kissed and teased him as he unlocked the door. "The coffee will be late this morning, and we only have an hour until April arrives."

He laughed. "If you give me an hour, I'm going to take it. Maybe we should say forty-five minutes, and I'll help you with the coffee."

"Okay."

He turned from the door and handed her keys to her. When she took them from his hand, he bent and scooped her up.

She gasped and gripped his shoulders, but laughed, too. "*Kade*? What are you doing?"

"Practicing," he said with a laugh as he carried her over the threshold and set her down. "For when we get married, and I carry you home."

He took her face between his hands and kissed her until she couldn't breathe. When he let go of her long enough to slip his hand into his pocket, she stilled. Her heart thundered in her chest. "You're asking me now?" she whispered. Just like that?

He grinned and bent to one knee. "Noelle Parker, will you marry me and make me the happiest man in the world?"

She put a hand to her lips as everything inside her trembled with excitement. "You're sure? How could you know so soon?"

He stood and met her gaze, his now serious. "I knew for certain the moment I thought I'd lost you. As much as I've been through, I still longed for a tomorrow. Without you, I realized there wouldn't be one. Marry me, Noelle. Please say yes."

"*Yes*." She touched his face and gave him a soft, lingering kiss. "Yes, Kade. I'll marry you. I could never live without you, either."

He crushed her to him and gave her another kiss that deepened into something more. Something so much more than she'd ever expected.

Something she'd savor for the rest of her life.

EPILOGUE

K ade cracked open the bottle of champagne. The sound of the cork popping brought cheers from the people attending the motel's grand opening.

Noelle glanced at the group composed of his family, Seth and April, and many others from Aspen, and she smiled. She couldn't imagine being any happier than she was at the moment. Except maybe when her wedding day arrived.

Kade grinned as he surveyed the crowd. "I'd like to thank everyone for coming. I wasn't sure I'd open this motel on time, but luckily, the heavens smiled down on me."

He glanced at Noelle. "I've been given more than I deserve. I'd like to dedicate this place to my lovely fiancée, and welcome you all to the Bluebell Inn. Eat as much as you'd like. Look around and explore the amenities. We'll offer discounted rates through the end of the year, so if you have family coming into town for the holidays, book now."

Kade took a sip of champagne and made his way to her, through a round of hearty congratulations and slaps on the back.

"You did it," Noelle said when Kade reached her. She

wrapped her arms around his neck and gave him a big kiss. "I'm very proud of you."

"And I'm very proud of you," he said.

She furrowed her brows despite the happiness flowing through her. "What for? I haven't done anything."

"You were smart enough to say yes to me." He grinned. "You obviously know a good thing when you see it."

"I do." She laughed. "I definitely do."

"Shall we mingle with our guests?" he said with a grin.

"Absolutely." She took his arm and walked happily toward the rest of her life.

I hope you enjoyed Noelle and Kade's love story. Read on for an excerpt from Crazy One More Time, the next in the Aspen Series.

Sign up for my newsletter to receive notifications of new releases, freebies, and special sales at www.CindyStark.com. Also, if you have a moment, I'd appreciate a review!

Thank you very much and happy reading!
   Cindy

PREVIEW: CRAZY ONE MORE TIME

1

A vivid blood-orange sun hovered close to the horizon as Corey Kendall approached the front door leading into Aspen's Town Hall. Evening shadows played on the sidewalks while lavender lilacs near the front of the building emitted a sweet perfume.

He stopped and held open the door, waiting for his parents to catch up. Before the city council meeting that night, he'd take an oath and become the newest representative of his small town. He'd be taking his father's spot on the council after health reasons had forced his dad to resign early.

Needless to say, Corey had been thrilled when the town had chosen him as a replacement.

As he waited, the sight of a woman exiting from the passenger side of a rusted blue pickup caught his attention. With silky blond hair and long legs peeking from beneath a fitted black skirt, she was a classic beauty against a piece-of-shit truck. Not unheard of in their part of the country.

The woman turned and leaned back into her vehicle, giving Corey a nice view of her ass. As an upstanding member of the community, he knew he shouldn't stare, but he did anyway. He was single. She appeared to be attractive. It made perfect sense in his world.

Corey's dad took hold of the door, gesturing for Corey's mother and him to step inside. "Come on, son. We need to get you sworn in before the regular meeting starts."

Generations of Corey's family had lived in Aspen, dating back to the late 1800s. Many had served their community in one capacity or another. Now it was his turn to leave a positive mark on the town as well. One that citizens could benefit from for generations.

A small group had gathered in the council's wood-paneled antechamber, including town dignitaries and family members. Corey made his way to the front of the room amidst warm smiles and congratulations, stopping when he stood before the town clerk. Mallory O'Brien's eyes lit with interest as she lifted a black, leather-bound bible and held it out in front of him.

She smiled then, her long, dark hair complementing sapphire eyes. "I'll add my congratulations, Councilman Kendall."

"Thank you, Mallory." She'd already celebrated his appointment with him when he'd taken her to dinner in Pinecone Valley the previous week. Polished and refined, she would fit in perfectly with his life's goals. He hadn't discovered that special spark between them yet, but they hadn't known each other for long.

She blinked her long-lashed eyes at him a few times, taking on a serious expression. "Repeat after me. I, Corey Jason Kendall, do solemnly swear to support the Constitution of the United States, the Constitution and Laws of the State of Utah, and the Laws and Ordinances of the City of Aspen, Utah."

He repeated her words before she continued. "I will, to the best of my ability, faithfully perform the duties of council member in the City of Aspen, Utah, during my continuance therein, so help me God."

Confidence, underscored by the need to do a good job, thudded inside his chest as he repeated the oath. Everyone in his long line of ancestors would smile today, including his parents. His dad had been so proud when the town had supported Corey's appointment, and Corey wouldn't let him down.

Larry Downs, the town's other council member, was the first to congratulate him following the brief ceremony. "Welcome aboard. Good to know we have another solid member of the community to protect our interests."

Corey returned his firm handshake, honored to be supported by a man he'd admired for many years. Time had threaded the older man's red hair with white, but his blue eyes still sparkled with intelligence and wit.

"That's right," Mayor Dwight Gardiner said as he, too, shook Corey's hand.

The mayor shared the same potbelly as Larry and Corey's father, though Dwight hadn't been lucky enough to hang onto much of his hair as he'd aged. "We can't let just anybody in the inner circle, you know. We need to ascertain whether a person will uphold our values, protect the better interests of Aspen. I think we've made the right choice."

Corey gave them a nod of reassurance. He wanted to remind the man that the citizens of Aspen had chosen him to serve, not the mayor, but he let it slide. Today was a day for celebration, and he didn't want to start out on the wrong foot. Not to mention, both men had hovered in the background of his childhood, and he'd enjoyed family outings with them and their families. He respected and admired them tremendously. "I'll do my best not to let you down."

"Of course you will," Dwight said with a wink. "Otherwise, we'd have picked someone else."

Again, an uneasy feeling slid over him, but Larry erased it with a friendly slap on the back. "Let's move this party into the council chambers. We have business to attend."

A group of over twenty Aspen citizens had already taken their seats in the small meeting room by the time they arrived. Corey followed his fellow council members inside and took a seat at the long table in front. Someone had placed a placard with his name in front of his seat, along with a crystal glass and a nearby pitcher of water.

He tried not to let the notion of power go to his head, but he couldn't deny he appreciated the prestige. Still, he'd silently vowed to always use his influence for the good of Aspen, and he meant to honor that.

His father sat in the front row alongside his mother, pleased smiles gracing their faces. For the most part, he'd been a dutiful son. He'd studied hard in school and had made good choices. He was proud of the respectable life he'd created. Besides his newest duties, he'd hung up a shingle a year ago, offering architectural services and had done well for a new business.

As Dwight welcomed everyone to the meeting, Corey scanned the rest of the faces, searching for the blonde he'd spotted earlier.

He found her in the back row sitting alongside old man Searle, and his heart faltered in surprise.

It couldn't be.

But it was. After all this time. The one person who'd thrown a wrench into his perfectly planned life. The one who'd tempted him to step outside the box. The one whose kiss he'd never forgotten.

Afton Searle.

Corey stared until her gaze collided with his and held for

several impossibly long seconds. His heart thundered in his chest with excitement. He hoped she would be happy to see him, but understood if she wasn't. Perhaps she still hated him like she had six years ago.

Then she smiled, and the world righted itself.

He could breathe again.

She looked different. No longer a skittish young colt, but a confident woman who held his gaze instead of sneaking shy glances at him.

Attraction coiled inside him like a sleek rattlesnake. He'd tasted her once, and her essence forever lingered in his blood. She wasn't a woman his parents would choose, but that wouldn't stop him from seeking her out now. He needed to know if her hold over him was real or a remnant of an overactive eighteen-year-old imagination.

Her grandfather leaned close to speak to her, and she turned her attention to him.

Johnny Searle looked every bit the outlaw in his old-fashioned suit, wearing a turquoise and silver bolero instead of a tie. He'd drawn his thinning hair into a ponytail, and Corey wouldn't be surprised if he packed a weapon beneath his suit coat.

Corey watched as Afton studied her grandfather's face, listening to him before whispering something in his ear. He'd never personally spoken to Johnny Searle, but his father had condemned the man on more than one occasion for his immoral ways. What those reasons were, had remained a mystery to him. Sure, Johnny had obviously lived a hard life, but many people in town liked him. Obviously, Afton did, if her expression was a sign.

Her smile could save the devil's soul. She'd been graced with a natural beauty he'd never been able to ignore. If their families hadn't come from such different backgrounds, he wouldn't have been so hesitant to approach her back then.

But the fates had thrown them together for one amazing night. He savored sweet memories of them tangled, naked on the grass beneath a star-filled summer sky. They'd made love and talked until almost sunrise, until his conscience had blasted him with guilt. If only he could keep that one snapshot of time and forget the rest.

They'd both just graduated from high school. He'd been dating straight-A, strait-laced Emily Clinton, but she'd been out of town. He'd reached the point, like he supposed all teenagers did, when he couldn't stand his parents' smothering ways, and he'd tapped into his rebellious streak.

Afton had been soft and willing, tasting of strawberries and her grandfather's whiskey. Unfortunately, a stiff shot of regret had followed. He'd never forgotten their time together. But the guilt of betraying Emily, not to mention his cold treatment of Afton the next morning, were times he'd rather leave buried.

Dwight banged his gavel, jerking Corey's attention to the present.

"Now that we've taken care of the housekeeping business, let's get down to the next item on our agenda. Johnny Searle, you have the floor for five minutes."

ABOUT THE AUTHOR

Award-winning author Cindy Stark lives in a small town shadowed by the Rocky Mountains. She enjoys writing about forever love with hot men and strong women in her sexy contemporary romances, along with penning unexpected twists in her emotional romantic suspense stories, and creating magical mayhem in her paranormal cozy mysteries.

She'd like to think she's the boss of her three adorable and sassy cats, but deep down, she knows she's ruled by kitty overlords. Someday, she hopes to earn enough to open a cat sanctuary where she can save all the kitties and play all day with toe beans and murder mittens.

Connect with her online at
www.CindyStark.com

ALSO BY CINDY STARK

ASPEN SERIES (Small Town Sexy Romance):

Wounded (Prequel)

Relentless

Lawless

Cowboys and Angels

Come Back To Me

Surrender

Reckless

Tempted

Crazy One More Time

I'm With You

Breathless

PINECONE VALLEY (Small Town Sexy Romance):

Love Me Again

Love Me Always

ARGENT SPRINGS (Small Town Sexy Romance):

Whispers

Secrets

BLACKWATER CANYON RANCH (Western Sexy Romance):

Caleb

Oliver

Justin

Piper

Jesse

RETRIBUTION NOVELS (Sexy Romantic Suspense):

Branded

Hunted

Banished

Hijacked

Betrayed

COOKIE CORNER COZY MYSTERIES (PG-Rated Fun):

Cookie Calamity

Haunted Cookies

Cursed Cookies

Conjured Cookies

SWEET MOUNTAIN WITCHES COZY MYSTERIES (PG-Rated Fun):

Midlife or Death

For Once in My Midlife

One Midlife to Live

Midlife in the Fast Lane

Midlife of the Party

Such is Midlife

Mysterious Midlife

Love of my Midlife

Merry Midlife

CRYSTAL COVE COZY MYSTERIES (PG-Rated Fun):

Murder and Moonstones

Brews and Bloodstone

Curses and Carnelian

Killer Kyanite

Rumors and Rose Quartz

Hexes and Hematite

TEAS & TEMPTATIONS COZY MYSTERIES (PG-Rated Fun):

Once Wicked

Twice Hexed

Three Times Charmed

Four Warned

The Fifth Curse

It's All Sixes

Spellbound Seven

Elemental Eight

Nefarious Nine

Hijacked Honeymoon

A Witch Without a Spell

Mystical Mayhem

OTHER TITLES:

Moonlight and Margaritas

Sweet Vengeance